## "I still have



"This can't go

quaking. "There's no future for

I could be in Cleveland next month. Or Toledo…" *Well, scratch Toledo.* The moment any decent spot came through, Julie was off. Leaving town. Leaving Ben.

A bittersweet feeling swept over her. Ben did generate sparks in her. Sparks she'd never felt with another man. Some of those sparks were incendiary.

His hand moved to the lapel of her robe. "You don't really need this. It's too warm in here."

Her gaze shot to the discarded clothing on the floor. Ben's eyes followed; then he looked at her. He knew she wasn't wearing anything under the robe. Leaning forward, he pressed his lips to her forehead, her cheek.

He was seducing her plain and simple, tempting her despite everything she had told him. He was banking on his sex appeal and charisma overcoming her resistance.

The walls were tumbling down.

*What resistance?*

Dear Reader

Talented Temptation author Elise Title has written another funny, sexy mini-series in the vein of the popular Fortune Brothers. The Hart Girls follows the ups and downs of three feisty, independent sisters who work at a TV station in Pittsville, New York.

In *Heartstruck*, Book 2 in the trilogy, fired news anchor Julie Hart has returned home to Pittsville. The only job she can find is hosting the local talk show—hardly the big time! But the airwaves start to crackle when she meets her gorgeous co-host, Ben Sandler!

You met Rachel Hart in *Dangerous at Heart*. Look for Kate Hart's exciting tale in *Heart to Heart*, available in October 1995. Happy reading!

The Editor
Mills & Boon Temptation
Eton House
18-24 Paradise Road
Richmond
Surrey
TW9 1SR

# HEARTSTRUCK

BY

ELISE TITLE

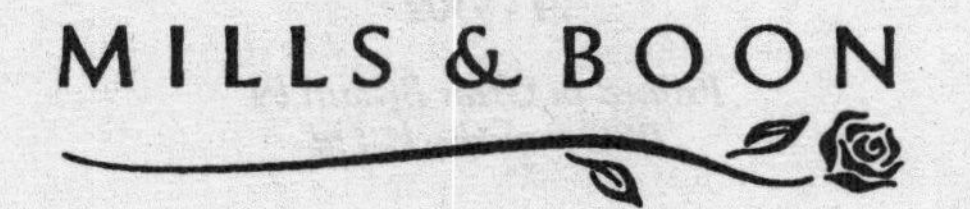

*All the characters in this book have no existence outside the imagination of the author, and have no relation whatsoever to anyone bearing the same name or names. They are not even distantly inspired by any individual known or unknown to the author, and all the incidents are pure invention.*


*First published in Great Britain in 1995*
*by Harlequin Mills & Boon Limited, Eton House, 18-24 Paradise Road, Richmond, Surrey TW9 1SR*



ISBN 0 263 79413 X

*21 - 9509*

*Printed in Great Britain by*
*BPC Paperbacks Ltd*

# Prologue

*July 11*

"Hot dog, summer in . . . Pittsville." In Mom's version it's "Summer in the City." One of those tunes from the Dark Ages that's supposed to capture the excitement of living in the city in the heat of the summer. Well, folks, this begins Skye Hart's second journal. And let me just say to begin with, that summer in Pittsville is a far cry from summer in any city. It's especially a comedown since this past spring here in Pittsville was so awesome, what with my Aunt Rachel getting accused of murder and my having to prove her innocence! With a little help from a pretty cool New York City cop, who ended up marrying my aunt after her acquittal. I think he would have married her even if she hadn't gotten acquitted. He would have probably helped her escape and they would have lived happily ever after in Mexico—I don't know what's happening to me lately; I'm getting all these romantic notions all of a sudden; it must be the heat.

The wedding was awesome. Everyone who is anyone in Pittsville came. Not that that's saying much. Things really got going when this stripper from Philadelphia who'd been a witness at the trial, showed up at the reception. Mom wouldn't let me see the "present" she gave the newlyweds, but from the way folks were snickering, and given the woman's chosen profession, I bet it had something to do with *s-e-x*. Really, grown-ups can be so . . . adolescent.

To be fair, life isn't as dull at the moment as it's been around the Hart "plantation" other summers, amazingly enough. For one thing, I got to be interviewed on TV—even if it was only on WPIT, the local Berkshire station owned by my mom. Still, it was the Ben Sandler show, "Pittsville Patter," which is WPIT's top-rated show. And the particular show I was featured on brought in the highest ratings in the station's history. Mom was beside herself with excitement.

The show was all about the Nelson Lang murder and my Aunt Rachel's brush with the law. Ben interviewed all the principals—as we call it in TV—involved: Aunt Rachel, Delaney Parker—okay, so at first I thought he was a hit man out to get Aunt Rachel after having done away with Nelson, but once I found out he was an undercover cop, you could say we worked hand in hand to prove Aunt Rachel's innocence. Before I go on, I just have to say how absolutely juvenile the kids in my school can be. The big joke is: "Where did Rachel Hart meet Delaney Parker? Undercovers!" Really. That is such a dumb joke. Delaney isn't doing undercover work anymore, anyway, now that he and Aunt Rachel are married and getting ready to have a baby. He's decided to put his roots down in Pittsville, which, if anyone asks me, isn't exactly the place I'd choose to put down roots. I'd want to be someplace exciting like L.A.

or Washington, D.C., or New York City. But who's asking me, right?

Anyway, where was I? Oh, right. My television debut. Well, not to brag or anything, but Ben's show wouldn't have been complete without my blow-by-blow account of how I practically solved the murder single-handedly and proved my aunt was innocent. A few kids at school actually asked for my autograph. Meg Cromwell, who does the local cooking show at WPIT, "Cooking with Cromwell," baked me a cake—carrot and rhubarb, ugh! But Mom says it's the thought that counts. Easy for her to say. She didn't have to eat a whole slice of that disgusting pinkish glop with Mrs. Cromwell's eyes glued to my mouth as I chewed and tried to smile and swallow at the same time.

The best praise for my efforts came from my Aunt Julie who told me my investigative skills were exemplary, and that one day I'd make a brilliant reporter. And she should know since she was, until very recently, the celebrated coanchor of "News and Views," a major network interview show taped in Washington, D.C. She and Jordan Hammond, her coanchor—and onetime lover; but more about that later—interviewed everyone on the show from the president's chief of staff to political rappers like Poli Sci—Poli Sci used to be one of my favorites but I've outgrown rap; now, I'm more into alternative rock. Aunt Julie would ask all kinds of probing questions of her guests. So would Jordan, but they sort of played it like good cop/bad cop. The way Aunt Julie described it to me was, Jordan was the charming, ingratiating one who'd wheedle things out of people by gentle persuasion. Aunt Julie was the one who didn't pull any punches. As Mom says, she didn't just interview people, she grilled them.

Unfortunately, it seems she grilled one influential bigwig too many on her show and ended up causing a major "brouhaha"—one of Grandpa Leo's favorite words and one I think is really neat. Mom says this was a case of Aunt Julie doing her homework too well and filling in a few too many blanks on a senator by accusing him of some extracurricular hanky-panky with several of his junior "staffettes," as Aunt Julie claimed he called them in private. He denied the charges even though she had proof positive, claimed she had publicly humiliated him, and demanded she make a full retraction on the air.

Let me tell you, this senator didn't know Aunt Julie. It's one thing if Aunt Julie made a mistake or got her facts wrong. Then, I can guarantee, she'd be the first to say she's sorry. Aunt Julie's got real integrity. Everyone in the family always says that about her. They say a lot of other things, too, some of which aren't exactly as complimentary, like, "She rushes in where only fools dare to tread." And, "This time she tripped and landed flat on her face." The first line is from Grandpa Leo; the second, from Mom. Aunt Rachel says that next to Mom, Aunt Julie's the most stubborn woman she knows. Which, if you knew my mom, is saying a lot!

Whatever anyone says about Aunt Julie, I say she's one tough lady. Instead of publicly apologizing on the next "News and Views" show—which, of course, we all watched with bated breath—she revealed a few more "titillating tidbits," as she called them, about the senator, and then wrapped up with this really fantastic speech about journalists having the solemn responsibility of informing the public about not only what's happening in the news, but what's going on behind the scenes. I confess, I had tears in my eyes. I was so proud of Aunt Julie. Mom and Aunt Rachel were a little teary, too, but they were also both looking at each other and shaking their heads. Grandpa Leo and his girlfriend, Mellie Oberchon, were at the house, watching the show, too. Mellie applauded Aunt Julie and then launched into this story about how her niece, Rona, once gave this rousing speech at the PTA about how certain parents were giving their children very unhealthy snacks while other parents were giving their kids healthy stuff like apples and raisins—yuk—and what was happening was that the kids were trading off. She was sure—Rona, that is—that this was causing a rampant increase in tooth decay. Mellie said certain mothers were irate but Rona stood her ground. Somehow, this was supposed to relate to Aunt Julie's situation. Aunt Rachel and Mom rolled their eyes when Mellie finished, but Grandpa Leo beamed at her. Whatever wavelength Mellie's on, Grandpa's obviously tuned in to it. I think it's kind of romantic—oops, there I go again.

To get back to the point, Aunt Julie's speech didn't just get a senator in a snit. It got her canned. And I guess word spread through the business—or as Aunt Julie says, the "industry"—because she's having one heck of a time finding another plum job in network news. The other night I walked into the kitchen to ask Mom to help me with a history assignment and she was talking to Aunt Rachel, who, I should mention, has blown

Mom's mind by turning into a top-notch sales manager for WPIT. Delaney's been a big help, too. Even though he's taken over Lyle Woodrum's post as Pittsville's chief of police, he used some of his big-city connections to help Aunt Rachel land some major sponsors. . . .

Anyway, before Mom noticed I'd walked into the kitchen—I guess I do make it a point to be kind of light on my feet—she was telling Aunt Rachel that Aunt Julie's been turned down for every job she's applied for, not only on the networks but even on cable. She said Aunt Julie's become a pariah in the business. I had to go look up *pariah* in the dictionary afterward. "*Pariah*—member of a low caste in southern India or Burma." Huh? I checked another dictionary that gave a second definition. "*Pariah*—outcast." Got it.

Poor Aunt Julie. As if losing her job and becoming a pariah wasn't enough, she also lost Jordan Hammond, her coanchor and the man she'd planned to marry. The night Aunt Julie arrived in tears on our doorstep, all she kept talking about was how Jordan had betrayed her. Oh, sure, she told my mom that Jordan claimed he went to bat for her, but she doesn't think he fought all that hard. And then after Aunt Julie got canned, he gave her this "song and dance" about how she really needed some time to "regroup," and how the last thing he wanted to do was "crowd her." Aunt Julie says to Mom, "Crowd me? He didn't call me for three weeks. And then it was just to find out if he'd left his gray cashmere jacket in my apartment. I took that jacket and cut it into neat little patches and mailed it back to him." Mom said, "Good for you." Then Aunt Julie started crying and Mom said her old standard, "No man is worth it." And Julie said, "You're right, you're right." Only then, she started crying even harder and saying she'd really thought Jordan was different from the others. And Mom started saying that once upon a time she thought Arnie—my dad, Mom's ex-husband—was different, too, only then she stopped talking because it finally dawned on her that I was next door in the kitchen—struggling with this dumb collage I had to do for art class—and I might be able to overhear what she was saying, which, obviously I was. Mom's always careful not to bad-mouth Dad when I'm around, even though she knows I know he cheated on her and divorced her to marry his girlfriend, Sue Ellen.

I worry about Mom sometimes. Okay, so my dad wasn't exactly a winner in the husband department and, I've got to admit, he's got his failings in the father department, too, but I do think Mom would be a lot happier if she didn't have to shoulder all of "life's burdens," as she calls them, by herself. Not that she thinks I don't help her. She's always saying we're a great team. And we are. But let's face it: I'm almost thirteen; I'll be in college in five years. Then she'll be all alone. I really think if Mom could find a good man, it would really perk her up and I would feel a lot better about going off and leaving her.

Right now, though, with Aunt Julie having man trouble, it only convinces Mom all the more that men can't be trusted. Delaney, she admits, is an exception to the rule, but Mom says it's usually the rule and rarely the exception that you can count on in this life.

I used to think Jordan Hammond was one of the exceptions, too. Last year, when I visited Aunt Julie in Washington, he was so nice to me—showed me all around the studio, even gave me a few pointers. But now, seeing how he dropped Aunt Julie just when she needed him the most, I totally agree with my mom—amazingly enough, since we don't agree on too many things these days—that he's a louse and not half the newscaster Aunt Julie is; and we even agree that Aunt Julie's better off without him. I think if she had a new anchor job to sink her teeth into, she'd forget about Hammond. Aunt Julie's so smart, so talented, so sharp, so pretty. If only she wasn't also a "pariah"!

Which brings me back to Ben Sandler, Pittsville's favorite newscaster and anchorman, not to mention producer, director and star of "Pittsville Patter." He came up with this great idea. At least every one—even me—thinks it's a great idea. Everyone, that is, except Aunt Julie, who thinks it's "the pits"!

Ben's idea is for Aunt Julie to team up with him on "Pittsville Patter" to do a kind of local version of "News and Views." Okay, so they wouldn't be interviewing presidential candidates or major rappers or anyone big-time like that, but Ben did have a state rep on the show last fall before the elections. And this past month alone he had on the mayor and the fire chief, who are pretty big officials for Pittsville. Ben's had on some wild guests, too. Like this very flamboyant cross-dresser and the local designer who did his/her outfits. It was just a fluke that Ben got them on the show. They had car trouble while they were passing through Pittsville on their way to Manhattan and had to hang around for a couple of days while their car was being fixed. Joy Thistle, who owns Thistle Boutique, met them while they were browsing in her shop and immediately called Ben, who's always on the lookout for interesting guests. Joy will look for any excuse to call Ben. She's got this mad crush on him, which makes her one of hundreds of Pittsville women whose hearts go thumpity-thump over the man. It's incredible how much fan mail he gets. And marriage proposals.

As for the cross-dresser show, it got the highest ratings until the "Hart family against the mob" show aired last month. And Ben got pretty good ratings when he had the football coach on his show last week, although the interview was cut short after the coach put his back out demonstrating a line pass or something and had to be carried off on a stretcher. He's still in traction down at Pittsville Medical Center.

Ben's show is doing great, but he's convinced the ratings for "Pittsville Patter" would skyrocket with Julie as his coanchor. He says it would add a real touch of "professionalism" to the show. And he thinks a lot of folks would tune in just to get a gander at Aunt Julie's legs. Aunt Julie accused him of being sexist and he accused her of not being able to take a joke.

The reason I know this is that I happened to be sitting in a booth having a soda with my friend Alice down at the Full Moon Café—which sounds kind of exotic but is just a plain old coffee shop—and Ben and Aunt Julie were in the very next booth, having this discussion. Well, I guess you'd say it was more a heated argument than a discussion. Aunt Julie went on to accuse Ben of wanting her on the show just to put her down a peg or two. She said he was just jealous that she'd made it to the networks and now he wanted her to have her "comeuppance"—whatever that means. Anyway, Ben said, "Your problem is, and always has been, that you take yourself too seriously." To which Aunt Julie replied, "Your problem is and always has been that you have no drive, no ambition, no aspirations." Ben grinned then—I know because I took a quick peek over the booth, ducking before I was spotted—and said in this real sexy voice—at least, Alice thought it was sexy; I thought he sounded like he had a frog stuck in his throat—"Give me half a chance and I'll share some of my most secret aspirations with you." To which Alice gave me this you-know-what-that-means wink and to which Aunt Julie said a few things that, if I wrote them down in this journal and my mother ever found it, she would have my head—and cut off my allowance for at least a year.

Alice says Ben's nuts about Aunt Julie and has been since grade school. She says everyone in Pittsville knows that he's never married because he's carried a torch for her all these years. I don't know about that, but I do know he sure has a knack for getting Aunt Julie all riled up. Right after their little get-together at the coffee shop, Aunt Julie came home in a really foul mood and told my mom that there was no way on earth that she would ever coanchor "Pittsville Patter" with Ben Sandler. "I'd rather work on a chain gang." Those were her exact words. I was right there behind the kitchen door when she said them....

# 1

"I MUST BE CRAZY," Julie muttered, checking herself out in the full-length mirror in WPIT's claustrophobically tiny greenroom—which wasn't green at all, but yellow. "Tell me I'm crazy."

Kate smiled, plucking a thread off the back of her sister's very smart-looking beige linen suit jacket. "You're not crazy. And you look positively glorious. You've got Couric and Pauley beat by a mile in the looks department."

Julie smoothed back her bobbed blond hair and checked her makeup. When she was sitting pretty at a national network, she had one of the best makeup people in the business to do her hair and face. Now she had to rough it. But only for a few weeks. Then, if all went well, she'd be on her way to Toledo to coanchor "Toledo Talks." Okay, Toledo wasn't Washington, D.C. It wasn't Chicago or New York or L.A., either. Still, it was a far cry from Pittsville. Even if WKSL in Toledo didn't have a network affiliation, at least it was part of the cable-news group. WPIT wasn't affiliated with anyone.

Instead of the usual butterflies she felt before going on the air, Julie felt a wave of depression. Sure, she knew she was going to have to work her way back to the top again, but she never dreamed she'd have to start over at rock bottom. She applied a bit more lip gloss, stepped closer to the mirror, wiped it off with a tissue. "Too orangy."

"Stop, already," Kate entreated.

"Okay, okay," Julie conceded. She knew it wasn't really her appearance that worried her. As critical as she was about her personal failings, she knew she was A-okay in the looks department—nicely defined features, clear ivory skin, gray-green eyes with tiny gold flecks, eyelashes so dark and thick that she didn't need mascara. Her hair could use another good cut, but it still looked stylish.

She pivoted to the side, sucking in a nonexistent tummy, and observed her slender, five-foot-seven figure in the mirror. She nodded at her reflection. She was holding her own, although she hadn't been working out since she'd left D.C. What went for a fitness center in Pittsville—a rowing machine, two stationary bikes, one StairMaster that was on the fritz, and two classes a day in step aerobics—was a far cry from the cosmopolitan, high-tech health-club facility she'd attended so faithfully for the past two years in the nation's capital. Dozens of work stations, Olympic-size pool, sauna, whirlpool, and a masseuse to die for. A few weeks without exercise hadn't done too much damage, though. She was still as trim and shapely as she'd been in D.C. and, Ben's sexist remark notwithstanding, she knew she had dynamite legs—her short, straight linen skirt and high-heeled pumps showing them off to good advantage.

"Do you want a soda? Something to eat?" Kate offered, grabbing a can of ginger ale from the small fridge in the room. "You've still got twenty minutes till air-time and you didn't eat a bite of dinner."

Julie shook her head distractedly, grabbing up a sheaf of papers from the dressing table near the mirror. She never ate before a broadcast.

"Julie, you've gone over those notes a hundred times," Kate said, popping the tab on the can of soda.

Julie looked up for a minute. "Diet?"

"What?"

"The soda."

"No. Why?" There was a faint edge of defensiveness in Kate's voice. "Do you think I need to drink diet soda? Do you think I'm putting on weight? Is that what you're saying?"

Julie waved her hand dismissively. "No. You know me. If I so much as look at anything with sugar in it, I put on a pound. And the camera puts ten pounds on you, as it is. Your weight is fine, Kate. You're robust. Healthy."

"Gee, thanks," Kate said dryly, then took a swig of soda from the can. "A little sugar won't kill me. Anyway, I don't believe in ingesting chemicals."

"Hmm." Julie was looking over her notes again.

Kate sidled over to the mirror. Taller and bigger boned than either of her sisters, not to mention older, she did know that as far as her physical appearance went she lacked Julie's fine-boned elegance and sophistication and Rachel's delicate, winsome beauty. Broad-shouldered, athletically built, with glossy shoulder-length brown hair that she wore pulled back from her face with combs, she accepted that she was attractive in a gal-next-door kind of way, but nothing to write home about. Then again, no one was writing home.

Julie put down her notes and looked over at Kate. "Ben did exactly five minutes of prep work for this interview. If he did that much, what with having to answer all his fan mail and tossing quips with the crew."

Kate turned from the mirror and took another swig of her soda. "That's Ben's style. Breezy, off-the-cuff..."

"You may call it breezy," Julie said. "I call it lazy, unprepared, slipshod..."

"Watch it, Julie, or you're going to give me a big head, throwing all those compliments my way," Ben said, popping his head in the door of the greenroom.

Wanting to avoid the inevitable fireworks that flared up whenever he and Julie were around, Kate slipped out of the room while Ben ambled in. As she closed the door, Kate couldn't help but experience a little shiver of alarm at the potential chaos that could reign when those two went on the air together. Kate wondered if this really was such a good idea. Still, there was no denying Julie had perked up since finally agreeing to go on the show. And if it was a disaster, it would most likely be over in a month. Julie had only consented to do four shows with Ben. She was supposed to hear about the coanchor job on "Toledo Talks" by the end of the month, and she was absolutely certain she'd land the spot. As she'd told Kate after sending in her impressive résumé, "They couldn't find anyone more qualified than me unless Couric wanted to give up the 'Today' show to be Frank Ingram's coanchor in Toledo. And if she did, it would be obvious she was having a nervous breakdown, so I'd land the job anyway."

As Kate headed down the hall to her office, she could still hear Julie and Ben going at it even though the door to the greenroom was closed. Oh, well, she thought, maybe the dynamic duo would get it all out of their systems before they went on the air.

THE WORDS, *Pittsville Patter,* were emblazoned across a folksy-looking barn-board backdrop, along the bottom of which was painted a hokey white picket fence and daisies. The tiny set consisted of two gray tweed swivel chairs—the second one newly added for Julie, but looking far from new—and a somewhat-threadbare brown corduroy sofa for the guests. Julie recognized the sofa as the one that used to sit in her sister Kate's living room. To the right was a rectangular-shaped multi-functional desk. At the moment a gingham cloth was draped over it, the top decorated with a vase of dried flowers. For local newscasts, the cloth was pulled off, the vase pushed to one side. For WPIT's newest show, "Shop till You Drop," the desk served as a display space for sundry goods ranging from cow manure to Pittsville Pirates T-shirts. Since the Pirates, Pittsville High's football team, had come in last place in the district the last four years running, there was an ample surplus of T-shirts for sale. Meg Cromwell's "Cooking with Cromwell" followed "Shop till You Drop." No problem. The top came off the desk, revealing a Formica counter and built-in stove.

Julie observed the makeshift set with despair. If anything else was needed to remind her how far from grace she'd fallen, this did the trick. Not that she was about to knuckle under. The first item on her agenda was to see to a total set change—that barn board had to go, as did the couch and swivel chairs, which needed to be replaced with solid-looking oak captain's chairs grouped around a substantial round table. And something had to be done about the lighting—what there was of it.

"Afternoon, Julie." A pert, slender, redheaded teenager came over and greeted her as she was surveying the set. "I'm Kelly. Ready for makeup?"

Julie stared at her blankly.

"I'm the makeup girl," the teen said brightly. "Well, actually I'm a senior at Pittsville High, but I work in the makeup department at JC Penney on Saturdays. And on Wednesday and Friday evenings, I do makeup for Ben and Mrs. Cromwell, and some of the others here at WPIT. Mrs. Cromwell, now she's a problem. Every time I make her up she insists I sample what she's going to cook on the show that night. I know a lot of folks are crazy about her concoctions, but between you and me, some of them can be really gross. Ben's great, though. I love doing his makeup."

She gave Julie a conspiratorial wink. "I mean, let's face it, you can't do much wrong with a face like his. I think he's positively gorgeous."

Julie was about to say that she didn't think he was all *that* gorgeous, but she didn't want to get into a debate over Ben Sandler's looks with this gal who was obviously gaga over the darling of the Pittsville airwaves. Teens. What did they know?

"Being gorgeous isn't a necessary criterion for a good investigative interviewer," Julie said archly.

Kelly grinned. "Yeah, but it doesn't hurt." Her grin faded as she gave Julie an openly assessing study. "Your nose is a little shiny. How about some powder?"

"My nose can't be shiny," Julie replied. "I've already done my makeup."

Gus, the short, oversize floor manager, as well as WPIT's carpenter and repairman, rushed onto the set. "Three minutes to air . . ."

The sleepy studio abruptly came alive with frenzied activity as the two cameras swung into position and cables started flying. Julie almost tripped, stepping back in an attempt to avoid Kelly's attack on her nose with a very large powder puff. Music started to blast.

"No, no!" Gus shouted into his headset as he began fitting Julie with her mike. "You're off cue. We've still got two minutes, two."

"What is *that?*" Julie gasped as the music thankfully stopped.

"The run-in theme for 'Pittsville Patter,'" Kelly said cheerfully as Gus rushed off to get another mike for Julie, since hers wasn't working. "Catchy little melody, don't you think?"

What Julie thought was not suitable for the teen's ears. "It sounds like a cross between 'Farmer in the Dell' and 'Lara's Theme' from *Dr. Zhivago,*" she said instead.

Kelly smiled. "Yeah. Great, isn't it? Mr. Russell, the music teacher at the grade school wrote it especially for the show. He's got lyrics, too."

Julie stared at her. "Lyrics?"

"Real catchy words, but Ben thought it might be too much. Poor Mr. Russell felt kind of bad at first, but then

Ben had Mr. Russell on the show and let him sing all eight verses with the elementary-school chorus. They were so adorable. The kids, I mean. Mr. Russell looks kind of like an owl. You didn't happen to catch the show, did you? It was on last fall. October, I think. Yeah, right before Halloween, because I remember all the kids were wearing their Halloween costumes. They looked so cute."

"Gee, and I missed it," Julie said, deadpan. Next on her agenda: new theme music. Even a Sousa march would be better. And she was going to ban school choruses for the next four weeks.

"Pitter, patter, what's the matter?" Kelly began in a flat, singsong voice.

Julie gave Kelly a dumbfounded look. "The matter?"

Kelly laughed. "Oh, that's the opening bar to the song. 'Pitter, patter, what's the matter? Pittsville Patter.' Get it?"

Julie's gaze shot around the set. "Where's Ben? We're on in—" she checked her watch "—a minute and a half. Where is he?"

"Oh, don't worry," Kelly said. "He always comes strolling in at the last minute. I dab a little powder on his face and put a comb through those gorgeous blond locks and he's set."

"I just don't understand what he's doing. Unless he decided to change his outfit, after all." Julie had pleaded with Ben to at least put on a jacket and tie, but he ignored her entreaty. Chances were, he wouldn't even roll down the sleeves of his denim shirt.

"He's probably schmoozing with Mr. Rockman," Kelly said, dabbing her powder puff across Julie's forehead. "Don't sweat it," she said with a little laugh.

Julie's head jerked up, the powder puff getting her in the eye. She blinked several times. "Schmoozing with Mr. Rockman? The head of the school board? The man we're interviewing in another—" she checked her watch "—sixty-five seconds?" Julie and Jordan had had an ironclad rule about never meeting with their guests before their shows. It took the edge off, gave away their advantage.

"Ben always likes to spend a few minutes with his guests before the show. And Mr. Rockman and Ben are old pals. They're on the same softball team. Go on fishing trips together." Kelly leaned a little closer. "When Mr. Rockman can get time off for good behavior."

"What do you mean?"

"My mom and Mrs. Rockman are friends. Well, they play bridge together. But Mom says Mrs. Rockman is real bossy, that she's the one who wears the pants in the family. What she says, goes. You know what I mean?"

Julie's eyebrow lifted. "Hmm. I think I do."

"Hello, beautiful."

Julie spun around at the sound of Ben's voice as he came up behind them. She was about to say something about his chauvinistic choice of address until she saw that he wasn't addressing her but Kelly, who simply beamed at the greeting.

His greeting to Julie was a playful wink, earning him a tight expression of disapproval in return—partly for the wink, partly because he hadn't even rolled down his shirtsleeves, much less conceded to her request for the jacket and tie.

Ben slid into one of the swivel chairs. The one, Julie noted, that was closer to the couch.

Ben caught her look. He knew just what she was thinking: that his was the number-one seat. "Hey," he said innocently, "if this seat would make you feel more comfortable . . ."

"I'm perfectly comfortable," she snapped. It took her a couple of seconds to realize he'd outfoxed her. She was slipping. Nerves. Okay, so maybe she wasn't so comfortable. How could she be expected to feel at ease and in command with a man who was impossibly unpredictable, and, worse still, took delight in infuriating her? A minute or so to airtime, and all she could think was, This was a *big* mistake.

"How's it going, Kelly? Did you ace that math exam on Monday?" Ben asked the doting young makeup girl as she dusted him with face powder.

"Got a B minus," she said, switching the powder puff for a comb. "But almost everyone else in the class got D's or failed." She quickly ran the comb through Ben's wavy blond hair, then stepped back and gave him a big smile. "Perfect," she said with adolescent sincerity.

"What do you think, Julie?" he said, turning her way. A provocative smile played on his lips.

What really got her goat was that he did look damn near perfect. "You could use a haircut." His hair was edging over the collar of his denim shirt, but the truth was, it looked good that way. She'd rather appear on the show naked, however, than admit that to him. Give a man like Ben Sandler an inch and you were done for.

"Thirty-five seconds to air!" Gus shouted, dashing over to the pair as Kelly scooted off. "How ya doing?" The question was addressed to the two of them at once.

Ben gave a thumbs-up sign as he clipped on his mike.

Julie slid into her seat, her new mike in place, and frowned. "This chair is too low."

Ben grinned. "You sound like Goldilocks."

"This chair is lower than your chair. By a good inch," Julie insisted, giving her coanchor a suspicious look. "You did this deliberately. You're always trying to put me down a notch. Now you've gone and done it literally."

"You're imagining things," Ben said. "Anyway, I offered you my chair, didn't I? If you feel at a disadvantage—real or imagined..."

"Oh, shut up," she snapped.

Gus gave the pair an uneasy look. "Twenty seconds..."

Ben reached across and tweaked Julie's knee. "Break a leg, kid."

She would have liked to break a leg, all right. Ben Sandler's.

"Jerry, lower the boom mike a little," Gus ordered as he stepped back toward the two cameras. "Lower. Lower..."

"Ouch," Julie muttered as the boom hit her square on the top of her head.

"Too low there, Jerry."

"Sorry," Jerry called out as Gus cued the technician in the control booth who punched a button. Gus held up five fingers, four, three, two, one...

Julie saw herself and Ben on the monitor as the dreadful theme music came on—mercifully lower than before—over which an announcer began the introduction.

"And now Carol's Cut and Curl on Market Street and Burtrell Plumbing and Heating on the Pittsville-Cranston line bring you the award-winning 'Pittsville Patter,' with none other than your favorite host and mine, Ben Sandler—"

The camera came in for a close-up on Ben, who gave a friendly little wave. Kelly, standing off to the right of the monitor, actually put her hand to her heart.

"And his new *hostess*, our own Kate Hart's kid sister, direct from a stint in Washington, D.C., Julie Hart. There's no place like home, right, Julie?"

Mortified, Julie was forced to grit her teeth and smile as the camera brought her in for a close-up and stayed there while the announcer finished with, "Their guest tonight, Alan Rockman, head of the Pittsville school board."

The instant they broke for a commercial, Julie swiveled around and glared at Ben. "Award-winning? Hostess? Kate Hart's kid sister? No place like home? Who the hell wrote that intro?"

Ben gave a little bow and smiled. "Not bad, huh? Had a nice, down-home touch, don't you think? Oh, and yes, I'm mighty proud to say that 'Pittsville Patter' did win an award a couple of years back."

"What award was that?" she asked dubiously.

"You ever heard of Emmy?" Ben asked offhandedly.

"Emmy? Give me a break, Sandler." Did he really think she was going to buy that they'd actually won an Emmy, the most coveted award in television?

"Emmy Hicks. She's the sweet little old lady from the Meadow Haven Retirement Home who emceed the WPIT awards show right there in the Meadow Haven rec room. 'Pittsville Patter' was voted, hands down, the most popular show on WPIT. We got a solid-gold-coated trophy and everything. Ask Kate. She keeps it on display in her office. Looks a little like an Oscar. Oscar Friedman from the hardware store, that is."

Julie shut her eyes. "I am crazy. What am I doing here? Why did I ever agree to spend even five seconds on the air with a man who has about as much business anchoring a news interview show as . . . as Captain Kangaroo?"

"Is the captain still on the air? Now, I always loved that show," Ben replied blithely to her barb.

"This is a nightmare," Julie muttered.

"This is show business," Ben corrected, wheeling his chair closer to her and planting a kiss on her cheek.

Julie glared at him. "Don't you ever—"

Something went *clunk* behind her. The ville in Pittsville had fallen off the barn-board backdrop. Gus rushed onstage with a hammer and a couple of nails. "No problem. No problem. Happens all the time."

Julie didn't doubt it.

Gus was driving in the last nail when they came back on the air. He gave a little wave to the camera as he scurried off. The ville in Pittsville was tilting downward.

As far as Julie was concerned, so was her life.

JULIE EDGED HER SEAT—which she was still absolutely positive was at least an inch lower than Ben's—closer to the sofa where the head of the school board was sitting, legs outstretched, arms relaxed at his sides. Ben had just spent most of their first ten minutes on the air more or less shooting the breeze with their guest. Julie took it all in, biding her time, waiting for the right moment to heat things up. The moment came when the school-board official mentioned the fiscal budget for the upcoming school year.

"About this new running track for the high school that you are proposing, Mr. Rockman," Julie remarked casually. "Doesn't that put quite a big dent in an already strained budget?"

Alan Rockman smiled edgily. He clearly saw her remark as coming from left field. "We're very excited about having a new track. I think it will pass without any difficulty." He deliberately didn't respond to her question, no doubt hoping she'd drop it. He clearly had never watched her on "News and Views."

"Is that right?" Julie countered. "You think this is really where the taxpayers of Pittsville want to see their hard-earned tax dollars spent? On a brand-new running track for the high school?"

The corners of Rockman's mouth twitched a little. He turned his gaze to Ben. "The boys and girls on our track teams are suffering because the track is so antiquated. Isn't that right, Ben? You run it all the time."

"It could definitely stand some work," Ben said amiably. "We all want to build up our leg muscles with a good jog, not break any bones tripping on a worn-out track."

Ben's eyes skidded by Julie's legs. "You must jog a lot, Julie."

"Not really," she said so tightly her lips didn't move at all.

Ben had to bite back a laugh. He could practically see steam coming out of Julie's ears. If only she could see that he was just trying to loosen her up a little.

Julie could feel her temperature start to rise. *I will not let him get to me. I will not lose my cool.* She swung around to Rockman, heard a strange pinging sound, and then emitted a gasp as her seat dropped another notch.

Her eyes—practically slits at the moment—shot over to Ben.

He held his hands up in denial that he had anything to do with it. Rockman chuckled. "Looks like you could do with a budget appropriation or two, yourselves."

It struck Rockman one sentence too late that he should have kept his mouth shut.

Julie turned on him like a warrior ready to do battle. She was fighting mad, even if the truth was, her fury had a lot more to do with her coanchor than it did with the head of the school board and a new running track.

"I've done some homework, Mr. Rockman, and I learned that if the track were to be repaired it would cost under ten thousand dollars. A new track would cost..." Julie paused deliberately and looked down at her notes. She knew precisely what the new track would cost. The pause was strictly for effect.

"Fifty-five thousand dollars," she said, zeroing back in on Rockman. "Don't you think there are other more worthy uses the Pittsville schools could put that money to? Like a full-time art teacher for the middle school? Or a guidance counselor for the high school? Or library expansion? Or any one of a dozen uses that would go toward improving the educational opportunities rather than the athletic facilities of our school system?"

Ben swiveled to face her. "Come on, Julie. You're not saying that athletics aren't an important part of getting an education? Why, I remember back in grade school, you were on the soccer team, the girls' softball team. I remember you even did a stint on the girls' basketball team. You were good, too. I bet you didn't know I was at a lot of your games."

"That's beside the point," she muttered. What was the point? That remark of his about being at her games when she was a kid threw her. What was he doing there? She tried to remember if his sister Leanne, who was in the same grade as her and one of her best girlhood friends, was on any of her teams. No. Leanne was into dance. She only did a short stint on the soccer team and quit after she sprained her ankle.

Ben was smiling at her. "You didn't know."

She could feel herself blush. In front of every viewer in the greater Pittsville area. And then, to add *injury* to *insult,* it was at that precise moment that the screw holding her seat in place decided to give way completely.

Ben saw it happening and reached out for her. His chair tipped in the process, and they both ended up entangled in each other's arms on the floor. The camera zoomed in for a close-up. There were muffled laughs from the crew.

Julie lost it. She swung at Ben, catching him right on the edge of his jaw.

"Aw, come on, Julie. You can't really think I'm responsible for that dumb chair coming apart?"

Julie was too busy feeling publicly humiliated to be thinking much of anything at the moment. She couldn't recall another single anchorwoman who'd collapsed with her coanchor on the floor during a show, much less one who'd ever struck her coanchor on the air. For the first time, she was truly grateful that "Pittsville Patter" was being aired on a hole-in-the-wall independent station.

Ben tried to help her to her feet. Julie refused his assistance. The seam on her skirt was ripped. She had a huge run in her panty hose. She looked desperately over at Gus. Surely it was time for a station break.

No such luck. They still had three minutes to go. It felt like an eternity to Julie.

"Here," Ben said gallantly, "you take my chair, Julie, and I'll join Al on the couch." Then he turned to the camera and smiled endearingly at his hordes of fans. "Just a few kinks we need to iron out, but Julie's being one heck of a sport. Not to mention that she's got one heck of a right hook. Of course," he quickly added, "we all know that sock was just an accident. Don't worry, Jules. No loose teeth."

Julie managed a sickly smile. Okay, so he got a point for trying to get her off the "hook" by lying about what he knew was a deliberate attack. Julie was equally certain that everyone viewing the show knew it, too. She was mortified.

Ben turned to Rockman and patted him on the shoulder. "Let's see. Where were we before things went a little haywire? Oh, yes, debating the pros and cons of a new track. You were saying, Al?"

Rockman cleared his throat. "A lot of people, besides the students, would benefit from having a new, safe track. We're hoping to encourage more people to come on out and do a little healthy jogging."

Two minutes to go before the break. Julie did her best to regroup. She smoothed back her hair and crossed her legs demurely at her ankles. And prayed that the chair she was now sitting on wouldn't go and collapse under her, too. "Does your wife jog, Mr. Rockman?"

The head of the school board's expression turned wary. "Why... yes."

"On the high-school track?" Julie persisted.

Rockman's eyes narrowed. "Sometimes."

"Wasn't Mrs. Rockman the one who initially proposed building a new track?" Julie was winging it on that one, but she had a gut feeling, thanks to her brief discussion with Kelly, the loquacious makeup girl, that she was on the right "track." Further confirmation came from Rockman's hostile look and the faint tittering of the crew. "Isn't this a case of whatever Lola wants, Lola gets, Mr. Rockman?"

"My wife's name is Rose," Alan Rockman said, his face red with fury and embarrassment. "This is the most outrageous..."

"Cut for commercial," Gus called out after signing them off.

The instant they went to commercial Rockman slapped his hand down on his thigh. "What is going on here, Ben? Since when did this show become a combination circus act/inquisition?"

"Now take it easy, Alan. Julie here's just feeling her way. She's had a pretty rough debut, what with her chair giving way and all."

"That has nothing to do with it," Julie was quick to disagree; quick to want to put the whole humiliating chair episode behind her. "The truth is, Rockman, everyone in town knows you do your wife's bidding—"

"Now, hold on, Julie," Ben broke in. "You go for every guest's jugular like you are Al's here, and pretty soon we're going to be running out of guests willing to come on the show."

Julie threw up her hands in disgust. "You're as spineless as he is."

"I beg your pardon," Rockman said indignantly.

Ben gave the school-board head's shoulder a little tap of assurance. "It's just first-show jitters."

Julie was beside herself. "Oh, you're impossible. This is impossible. This show isn't about raising issues, airing views, getting at the heart of what's really going on."

Ben grinned. "Now you're catching on. But, hey, I don't mind a little on-screen dueling. You always were my pick for a debate opponent. Only watch that right hook of yours. You swing at me on every show and we're going to start losing our male viewers. Unless, of course, I swing back," he teased.

Julie had to fight the urge to take another swing then and there. The only reason she didn't was because the stage manager was doing the countdown. "Five, four, three, two, one . . ."

It was only when they got back on the air again that either one of them noticed that their guest was nowhere in sight. Gone. Vanished. No other guests were scheduled, and they still had ten minutes of airtime to get through.

*August 3*

What a show! We were all watching Aunt Julie's debut from the control booth—me, Mom, Aunt Rachel, Delaney. It was better than any sitcom I've seen. I mean, when Aunt Julie and Ben fell on the floor together and then Aunt Julie punched him, we all started laughing so hard, tears were running down our cheeks. Mom kept saying, "It isn't funny. Poor Julie." Only she couldn't stop laughing any more than the rest of us. And then there was Mr. Rockman going berserk when Aunt Julie made that "Lola" crack.

The best, though, was the last part of the show, after Mr. Rockman stormed off and Aunt Julie and Ben had to wing it. Aunt Julie looked kind of panicky at first, but Ben was real laid-back like always and started chatting about the nice work Mel Wills, the contractor, had done on the new town hall and how the Pittsville Garden Club had done a terrific job on the flower beds on the green this summer. "Come to think of it, we haven't had the garden club on yet this season. We'll have to fix that," he said.

Aunt Julie was just staring at him like he'd lost his marbles or something as he kept on chatting away. All of a sudden she said to him, "Is this all you can talk about?" And he just smiled at her and said he'd talk about anything she wanted to talk about. Aunt Julie looked stumped. But only for a few seconds. Then she launched into an attack on the new Minimart mall that some developer wants to build on the south side of Pittsville. She went on about how it would affect the ecology of the whole south side of town, and that it was too close to the wetlands, and on and on, getting more fired up by the minute. Ben, meanwhile, was all for the mall, saying as how it would boost Pittsville's economy by providing more jobs. And that's when the fireworks started. They started arguing back and forth, and pretty soon they weren't fighting over the pros and cons of the mall anymore but Aunt Julie's chair, and the set, and the guests. And then Ben got her really steamed when he told her, right on national television—well, okay, *local* television—that the reason he went to all those ball games she played in back in elementary school was that he had a secret crush on her.

Aunt Julie turned beet red. And that's when she slugged him again, just before the show went off the air.

The phones at the station have started ringing off the hook—we've got six phones now because of our "Shop till You Drop" show.

Meanwhile, Aunt Julie's locked herself in the greenroom.

# 2

"JULIE, PLEASE OPEN the door," Kate pleaded.

There was no response.

Rachel tried next. "Listen, Julie, the viewers loved the show. We must have logged in a hundred calls so far and the phones are still ringing. Only one negative caller in the batch. And that was from Agnes Pilcher, naturally." Agnes was Kate's ex-mother-in-law. She disapproved of every show on WPIT. She disapproved of how Kate ran the station. She disapproved of Kate, period. Before Arnie divorced Kate, he was in command of WPIT. With a lot of input from his ultraconservative mother. Kate, however, ended up with the station as part of the divorce settlement, leaving Agnes out in the cold. Now all she could do was complain and criticize, which she did in spades that night.

"You were a big success, Aunt Julie," Skye piped in. "I've never told anyone this, but I always thought 'Pittsville Patter' was kind of boring. So did most of my friends." Which was true, except they watched the show anyway just because they were all wild about Ben Sandler. To Skye, who'd known him since she was born, Ben was more of a big brother. She never really saw what the fuss was all about.

"The show tonight was anything but boring," Skye went on. "I really thought it was great. I thought you were great. And none of us blame you one bit for socking Ben. Either time."

Ben, who had joined the others outside the greenroom, gave Skye a friendly nudge. "Thanks a lot, kiddo."

Kate jiggled the door handle. "Please, Julie. It's getting late. You must be exhausted. We're all exhausted. . . ."

"I'm not the least bit tired," Skye said.

"You're not helping matters here," Kate told her daughter, then resumed her entreaties to her sister. "How about, instead of staying at Dad's place while he and Mellie are in Connecticut, you come back home with me tonight and we'll talk it all out? We can stay up all night if you want."

There was still no response. Kate and Rachel shared worried looks.

"You don't think she'd . . . do anything . . . stupid?" Rachel murmured anxiously.

"You sure you can't find the key, Kate?" Ben asked.

"You know we never lock anything but the front and back door at night. The key could be anywhere. It could take me hours to find it, if I could find it at all."

"We can always break the door down," Delaney suggested.

"No. Wait," Ben said. "I have an idea. I bet I can get in through the window."

"We're on the second floor, Ben," Kate reminded him.

"I'll climb out the window in the storage room next door and just shuffle along the ledge to the window of the greenroom."

Before anyone could talk him out of it, he dashed off.

Kate, Rachel, Delaney, and even Skye, shared looks. They were all thinking the same thing: What if Julie pushed Ben off the ledge?

JULIE KNEW IT WAS ridiculous to hole up in the greenroom like that. It was just that she couldn't bear to face anyone. If only the floor had opened up beneath that god-awful set and swallowed her right up. Her career was over. She had gone from anchorwoman to clown in the course of a half hour.

She paced the room, catching sight of her reflection in the mirror—the split seam in her skirt, the huge run in her panty hose, her face all flushed. She looked like she'd spent the past half hour in a street fight instead of on a television show.

Well, it had been more like a street fight than a television show.

Oh, he made her so mad. First that damn chair collapsing—and she didn't believe for one minute that Ben had nothing to do with it, no matter what he said—and then that damn crack about having had a crush on her in grade school. A lie. She knew it was an absolute lie. He'd never given her so much as a second look in grade school. It was probably Samantha Warner or Lizzy Carson whom he'd come to watch play. They were the two most popular girls back then. And they both were crazy about Ben. Practically every girl in the school had had a crush on Ben. Not her, though. Never. Ever. Well...maybe for an irrational moment or two...back in the third or fourth grade. Okay, and maybe for a couple of days when she was a sophomore and he was a senior in high school. A few mad moments.

Ben Sandler had certainly never had a crush on her, though. He used to tease her unmercifully when they were growing up. They were always getting into arguments. He used to call her pigheaded, stubborn, opinionated. She called him a few choice names herself. Some crush.

Julie was sure he'd just said that on the show tonight to turn her into a complete laughingstock. Then she had to go and make it worse for herself by resorting to physical violence. For the second time. Which made that two times in her whole life that she'd ever struck a man! She'd certainly made up for lost time in one fell swoop. Or two fell swoops, as it were.

Oh, that man made her so mad. Even getting summarily dumped by Jordan Hammond hadn't gotten her this livid. What was it about Ben Sandler?

There was a rap on the window. She spun around only to come face-to-face with the devil, himself. For a moment, she was too stunned to speak. Weren't they on the second floor? The man was positively nuts. Not that that was any surprise.

"Go away!" she shouted at him.

Ben tried to push up the window, but it was stuck and he didn't have much maneuvering space, given that he was standing on a ten-inch ledge. And he wasn't all that crazy about heights.

Julie rushed over to the window looking for a way to lock it, but there wasn't one. She put her hands on the sash of the large bottom pane so he wouldn't be able to lift it.

"I mean it, Ben. Go away. I never want to see you or your dumb show again. I'm through. I would rather walk a tightrope over Niagara Falls than appear on TV with you ever again in my lifetime."

Ben was not particularly keen on having this discussion with Julie while standing out there on a ledge a good twenty feet off the ground. "Okay, fine. Just let me in."

"You can get back in the same way you got out there."

"Jules, you've got your whole family worried about you."

"I'm fine. There's nothing to worry about. You go tell them I'm fine. I just want to be left alone for a while."

"Is it still the chair? Look, I swear—"

"Oh, shut up," she said, turning her back on him.

The instant she did, she heard him cry out. She spun back around and stared out the window. He was gone.

"Oh my God!" she cried, her hand flying to her mouth. Then, quickly, she leveraged all her weight to lift up the jammed window, and stuck her head out and down, fully expecting to see Ben splayed out on the ground.

"See, you do care."

Her head jerked to the right. There he was, pressed against the wall, not a foot from her. Before she had time to react—maybe time to push him off the ledge, judging from the look on her face—Ben swung around, gripped the window frame and pushed his way into the room.

"Now Jules, let's sit down and talk this over rationally like two mature people—"

"There aren't two mature people in this room," she said tightly.

He gave her an aw-shucks smile. "Come on, Jules, just because you acted a little adolescent on the show..."

He grabbed her hand before she could swing at him again. "I really hate you, Ben."

"Then why'd you look so scared when you thought I'd fallen off the ledge?"

"I wish you had fallen," she muttered.

He started toward her. "No, you don't, Jules."

"And don't call me Jules," she snapped, stepping back with each step he took closer.

He kept coming toward her. "I've been calling you Jules since you were in kindergarten."

"And you knew I didn't like it then." She stumbled over the back of a chair leg and started to fall backward. Ben lunged for her, catching hold of her in the nick of time.

Julie, however, was far from grateful. "Let go of me!" she shrieked. "I mean it, Ben. You let go of me this instant or I'll..."

"Fine," he said, releasing his grip. She wasn't expecting him to oblige so quickly and nearly landed on the floor anyway. Fortunately, she grabbed onto the back of the chair and righted herself.

They stared at each other in silence. Tears edged over Julie's eyelids. She turned her head away.

"I really think we have something here, Jules," he said softly. "The viewers really ate it up."

"At my expense," she muttered, close to the breaking point and damned if she was going to give Ben Sandler the satisfaction of witnessing it. She sank into the chair.

"No, you've got it all wrong," Ben insisted. "The viewers thought you were terrific. You should have been on the line with them. They thought you had fire, gumption, spirit. They raved about you, Jules. Turns out you were right on about the taxpayers not wanting to see their hard-earned bucks getting spent on a new running track. And at least half of them agreed with you about the Minimart mall."

"What about . . . the rest of it?" she mumbled.

Ben knelt down in front of her. He cupped her chin, tilting her head up. "Quite a few thought I deserved to get slapped."

The desire to burst into tears started to abate. "Both times?"

A boyish smile played on his lips. "I'd say a few thought it was overkill, but then there were those who definitely felt I had it coming to me."

"Well . . . you did."

"I always was a sucker for that feisty quality in you, Jules," he said gently, his hand reaching out, tentatively smoothing her hair away from her face.

Julie saw the glitter in his blue eyes, the seductive smile on his lips. She knew precisely what was on his mind. The problem was, it was on her mind, too. She'd known Ben Sandler twenty-three years—ever since she was five years old. In all those years, they'd never kissed. Never once. Why should they? Why would they? Why, indeed!

His gaze rested on her mouth. She could feel his fingers sliding lightly down her hair, causing her pulse to beat erratically when they arrived at the sensitive skin at the nape of her neck.

"No, Ben," she murmured, but neither one of them took her protest to heart as his face came toward her. She felt the moist heat of his mouth closing on her lips, the insinuating movement of his tongue against her teeth. Her lips parted.

This wasn't fair. He was getting her at a weak moment. Her whole personal and professional life was in collapse. She was feeling so vulnerable. Her resistance was low. He looked so damn good. Those eyes. That smile. Those lips. Those incredible lips.

His hands slid down her back. Her arms wound around his neck. Their tongues met. Julie's heart raced. A kiss twenty-three years in the making. Just her luck: It would go and have to be worth it! Neither of them was in any hurry to end it.

Which was eminently obvious to the group who burst through the door. Her two sisters, her brother-in-law, her niece, and Gus, the stage manager—who'd dug up the lost key—stood there, agog.

Julie shoved Ben away, mortified—yet again. Caught kissing the enemy. As if she hadn't suffered enough humiliation for one evening. Well, at least it hadn't happened on the air. Small consolation . . .

"SO YOU KISSED HIM. It isn't a crime," Kate said as she watched with amazement as Julie dug into the quart container of Ben and Jerry's Double Dutch Chocolate ice cream in their father's kitchen later that night. She'd nearly emptied it. This, the sister who couldn't even look at anything with sugar in it. Proof positive that Julie was going over the edge.

"I did not kiss him. He kissed me," Julie snapped, scooping up another spoonful of ice cream and stuffing it into her mouth.

"I've always thought Ben was very attractive," Rachel offered, nibbling on some cold chicken. Her ravenous appetite since the start of her pregnancy was nothing new. "And everyone knows he's had a crush on you for years and years."

Julie's head jerked up. "He has never had a crush on me. I don't care what 'everyone knows.' Don't you think I'd know if someone had a crush on me? Well, don't you?" she demanded, her gaze shifting from Rachel to Kate, then back to Rachel again.

"Sorry," Rachel demurred. "I didn't mean to upset you more, Julie."

"I'm not upset. I was upset when I first walked out on that ridiculous set tonight."

"I agree. The set could definitely use some updating," Kate quickly conceded. "I'd love your input."

Julie wasn't listening. "I was upset when the *ville* in *Pittsville* fell down. I was upset when the stage manager was still nailing it up after we went back on the air. I was upset when I sat there listening to Ben do his pathetic imitation of a probing interview. I was upset when my chair fell apart."

She waved her spoon at her two sisters. "When Ben fell on top of me on the floor, then . . . then I definitely moved beyond 'upset.' I've been moving beyond 'upset' ever since. Above and beyond 'upset.' I am now so far above and beyond 'upset' that merely feeling 'upset' would actually be a relief. I'd welcome it. I'd be thrilled to be just 'upset.' Perfectly thrilled."

Throughout her diatribe she kept downing spoonfuls of ice cream so some of her words were garbled, but her two sisters heard enough to catch the drift. When she finished, the ice-cream container was empty.

Julie rose abruptly and stormed over to the refrigerator, pulling open the freezer door. "Is that all the ice cream Dad has in the house?"

"I think he might have some . . . cookies in the cupboard," Rachel offered tentatively. Kate nudged her. She knew Julie was going to hate herself in the morning for consuming all those calories.

Rachel got the message. "Maybe not. I think he's out. Yes, I'm sure of it. No cookies."

Julie stood there, staring into the freezer compartment. "What am I doing? I never eat ice cream. I don't even like ice cream. I probably just put on ten pounds."

She turned slowly around to face her sisters. "Only, you know what? I don't really care. After all, what difference does it make? My career is shot. I've made a public spectacle of myself. There's every possibility someone from "Toledo Talks" will get a tape of the show. Can you imagine them hiring me now? Not unless they needed—" her voice broke "—comic relief."

"Oh, Julie," Kate and Rachel said in sympathetic unison.

Julie shuffled over to the pine kitchen table and sank into a chair, dropping her head in her hands. "Why did I do it?"

Rachel and Kate gave each other puzzled looks. Which "it" did Julie mean?

"I don't even find him all that attractive," Julie mumbled into her hands. "Well, I guess, impartially speaking, I'd have to say he's attractive, but he's certainly not my type of 'attractive.' He dresses like a farmer, his hair is way too long, he's built too . . . too broad. He completely lacks ambition. His views on things . . . Well, I don't really think he takes anything seriously. He certainly doesn't take me seriously. And he always seems so damn sure of himself."

"What about Jordan?" Rachel asked. "Wasn't he sure of himself?"

Kate scowled at Rachel. She didn't think bringing up an ex-lover who'd dumped Julie was going to help matters any.

Julie did lift her head up. "Jordan?" She'd been so preoccupied with Ben, she hadn't given Jordan Hammond a thought all evening. A record.

"Jordan is so completely different from Ben," Julie said adamantly. "He's sophisticated, polished, well traveled. . . . I bet Ben's never even been out of the country."

"Not true," Rachel said. "He's got this picture of himself and . . . someone . . . right in front of the Eiffel Tower in Paris."

"What someone?" Julie asked, then quickly added, "Not that it matters in the least. I don't really care. . . ."

"Samantha Warner," Rachel said.

Julie shot her kid sister a look. "Samantha Warner? Our. . . Samantha Warner?" She knew it. Didn't she just know it? Samantha Warner. He'd had a crush on her since grade school. "I thought Samantha was married. Didn't she marry some lawyer from Connecticut?"

"They got divorced," Kate said.

Julie toyed with the sugar bowl shaped like a cow on the table. "And was that picture taken before, during, or after the divorce? Not that it matters . . ."

"After," Kate said. "And I'm sure this doesn't matter to you, either, but they didn't go to Paris together. Ben went there alone. If you ask anyone who knows Samantha, they'll tell you she followed him over there with the definite goal of seducing him."

"Didn't Samantha always have the hots for Ben?" Rachel asked Kate.

"Ever since I can remember," Kate replied. "And it drove her crazy that he never did fall at her feet like almost every male in Pittsville. I remember when she won the Miss Plum Tomato pageant in town, she was fit to be tied that Ben made up some excuse for not taking her to the after-pageant ball."

"So . . . what happened?" Julie asked idly.

Kate frowned. "Hmm. I think she ended up going to the ball with Doug Tyler."

"I don't mean the ball. I mean . . . Paris."

Kate fought back a smile. "Paris? Oh, you mean Ben and Samantha."

Julie seemed intent on trying to arrange the paper napkins neatly in the napkin holder next to the sugar bowl.

"I don't really know for sure," Kate said.

"Well, it's . . . pretty obvious, I'd think," Julie muttered. "Why else would he keep that picture of the two of them on his desk? Not that it matters," she hurried to add.

"Right," Kate agreed.

Rachel nodded.

Julie regarded them both with a resolute expression. "I don't give two hoots for Ben Sandler. And furthermore, I'm through with anchormen. I'm through with men, period."

Kate grinned. "Now you're talking."

Rachel sighed. "It's just too bad there aren't more guys like Delaney to go around."

"Right," Kate and Julie said in unison.

Julie put her elbow on the table and dropped her chin into the palm of her hand. "I'm going to put this nightmare of a night behind me. I'm going to pretend it never happened. I'm even going to try to forget—"

"The kiss?" Rachel asked.

Julie scowled. "The quart of ice cream I devoured."

Rachel patted her gently on the back. "It's going to be okay, Julie."

"Sure it is," Kate seconded.

"And the kiss."

Kate and Rachel grinned.

Julie managed a half smile. "Well, I've kept you both up late enough. Let's all get some sleep."

"Good idea," Rachel said. "And you'll see. Tomorrow things will look altogether different to you."

Kate smiled at her kid sister who was ever the optimist, then patted Julie on the shoulder. "Well, at least they may not seem as awful as they do now."

"No, really, I feel better already. I told you, I'm putting it behind me," Julie insisted as she walked them to the kitchen door and saw them out. After they were gone, she leaned against the closed door for a few moments, then dragged herself into the living room. She switched on the VCR and ran back the tape she'd recorded, all the while telling herself it would only make her feel worse. But she had to see for herself.

She pressed Play.

"And now, ladies and gentlemen, 'News and Views,' with our distinguished anchors, Jordan Hammond and Susan Smith. Tonight, their guest will be Senator Dan Ruttencutter from Nebraska. . . ."

There she was. Susan Smith. Her replacement. Blond, slender, polished, well-informed, with a Bostonian twang, wearing a Kamali suit that was practically a duplicate to one she owned.

There she was. Sitting in *her* chair. Next to *her* man. Interviewing *her* guest. A few pointed questions. Some gentle barbs. The senator squirmed a little.

She watched the whole show through, hoping . . . Hoping for what? That Susan Smith's chair would collapse? That the *Views* in *News and Views* would fall off and conk Susan Smith on the head? That Jordan would say something outrageous to his new coanchor and she'd wind up and sock him in the jaw?

No such luck. Jordan was ever the charming and gracious coanchor. He and Susan seemed to be working very well together. If he missed his old anchor even a little, he certainly gave no hint of it on the air.

The tape turned to static at the end of the show. After a few seconds, the picture cleared. The end of a toothpaste ad came on. Then that dreadful theme music . . .

"And now, Carol's Cut and Curl on Market Street and Burtrell Plumbing and Heating on the Pittsville-Cranston line bring you the award-winning 'Pittsville Patter,' with none other than your favorite host and mine, Ben Sandler. . . ."

Only then did Julie remember that she'd also taped "Pittsville Patter" that night. She started watching. Maybe it wasn't as awful as she imagined. How could it be as awful as she'd imagined?

After the show finished, Julie knew how.

# 3

"YES, I UNDERSTAND.... I just thought that I could fly out to Toledo and we could... touch base. It wouldn't have to be a formal interview.... Yes, right. I see your point, but..."

Julie twirled her finger nervously around the telephone coil as she listened to some snot-nosed producer from "Toledo Talks" giving her the bum's rush.

"But I can expect to be hearing from you within a couple of weeks?"

She scowled. "More like three or four? Isn't that cutting it awfully close?"

The producer didn't appear to think so. Julie hung up and sank back against the pillows of her old childhood bed. Tears brimmed in her eyes. They weren't going to hire her. She knew it. And since there was no way they could have gotten their hands on a tape of her humiliating debut appearance on "Pittsville Patter" yet, this had to be more fallout from her fall from grace at "News and Views."

That whole debacle still made her so mad. So indignant. She hadn't done anything wrong. It was no big secret that Senator Russell Cooper was a sleaze. All she'd done was let his constituents and a few million other viewers in on what everyone in D.C. already knew. She was just doing her job. And as far as she was concerned, doing a top-notch job of it.

The irony was, she was out of a job—or, from the looks of it, out of a career—and that sleaze Cooper was very likely to get reelected. It wasn't fair. It wasn't equitable. Unfortunately, it wasn't going to change anything to lie there and moan about it.

She looked around her old bedroom with its striped blue, gray and white wallpaper, the red-and-white Pittsville High banner over her bureau, the shelf by the window displaying four debating trophies—two from high school, and two from Smith College where she'd gotten her journalism degree. Nothing in the room had been changed since she was a teen. A teen filled with so many hopes and dreams. So much determination. She was going to make it in network news. She was going to be one of the top women anchors in the business. Nothing was going to stop her.

Nothing but her big mouth.

It had been years since she'd spent any time up here in the bedroom of her youth. Now she was back again, house-sitting while her dad and Mellie visited friends in Connecticut for a few weeks. Her return to the old homestead was strictly temporary, she was quick to remind herself, some of her optimism resurfacing. Something, somewhere would come through for her. It had to. She had talent, brains, drive, determination. And, okay, a damn good pair of legs. Maybe that producer from "Toledo Talks" was just having a bad day.

One thing was certain: There was no way on earth Julie Hart was going to stick around Pittsville for the rest of her life. Even the rest of the month felt intolerable. And she'd adamantly made up her mind that under no circumstances was she going to coanchor three more "Pittsville Patter" shows with Ben. She simply could not risk any further humiliation. Okay, she admitted to herself, she also didn't want to risk any further encounters with Ben Sandler. She still wasn't able to get that kiss out of her mind. What had come over her? Why was she still thinking about it? About him?

She reached for her purse and pulled out a snapshot of Jordan Hammond. The only one she had left. She'd ripped up all the others. Somehow, when it got to this last one, she couldn't bring herself to destroy it. *Thanks for the memories. Well, some of them, anyway.*

She studied the photo dispassionately. There was no question Jordan was a handsome man. The perfectly coiffed short dark hair had the tinges of gray at the temples—she'd been disillusioned to discover those gray hairs weren't natural; he'd had them done by his hairdresser because he thought it gave him an air of distinction. His expression was serious—almost somber—as he gazed out at the camera. He was a man with important things on his mind, a man who exuded intelligence. Only Julie knew that he hadn't exactly distinguished himself at the University of Ohio, almost flunking out in his junior year. Not that he'd confessed that to her; she'd just happened to spot his college transcript in a file in his desk. Okay, so she'd been doing a little snooping. Their relationship was starting to get serious and she didn't want to be surprised by any skeletons in his closet. Or in his desk drawer.

She slipped the photo back in her purse, her mind drifting to Ben again. Funny, how he'd never come across as particularly brainy, when, in truth, Ben had graduated summa cum laude from Amherst College. Whatever else she might say against Ben, she couldn't deny he was damn intelligent. Which made it even more frustrating as far as Julie was concerned. How could a guy with his brains, his looks, his . . . charisma—even she, in a very weak moment, had succumbed to it—settle for being the big fish in what amounted to nothing more than a tiny fishbowl? With any drive at all, he could make it to the big leagues.

The doorbell rang downstairs. Julie glanced over at the clock. It was nearly noon and she was still in her nightgown. She figured it was probably Kate at the door, doubtless prepared to give her another pep talk.

Julie groaned as she got out of bed, her hand going to her stomach. How could she have eaten a whole quart of ice cream last night? She heard something crinkle under her foot. The corners of her mouth turned down as she spied the empty cellophane bag. And all those taco chips . . .

"Coming, coming," she shouted irritably from the stairs as the doorbell rang again.

No sooner had she opened the door than she was trying her best to shut it again.

Ben wedged his foot against the doorjamb. "Hey, I want to show you something."

"Go away."

"You look awful," Ben said cheerily.

"I feel awful," she snapped, hating the fact that he, on the other hand, looked disgustingly robust. Why not? He had no sorrows to drown.

Ben's foot didn't budge. "Well, I brought something over that's going to make you feel a whole lot better, Jules."

She gave him a rueful survey. "It isn't your head on a platter, so I'm not holding out any great hopes."

When she reluctantly stepped aside she saw the huge mail sack at his feet. He lifted it up, swinging it over his shoulder, Santa Claus fashion, and started whistling the theme music to "Pittsville Patter," of all things, as he stepped inside the cool Victorian vestibule.

Julie's hands went up to her ears and she demanded he cease and desist before she clobbered him over the head with her father's umbrella, which was hanging on the coatrack.

His blue eyes sparkled. "Are you always grumpy in the morning?"

"It's almost afternoon and yes," she said flatly.

"How about some coffee? And some scrambled eggs and bacon?"

"This isn't a restaurant, Ben. And I hate to cook."

"No," he said. "I'll cook. You eat. And read," he added, his gaze shifting to the mail sack.

"What is all that?" she demanded as he carted it down the hall to the kitchen at the back of the house.

He turned back to her and grinned. "Fan mail. And these are just the phone messages written down from our callers. I expect the letters will be pouring in by tomorrow."

"I don't want to read them," she said stubbornly. "Living through it was bad enough. I don't need to be reminded." She had to shout because he'd already disappeared into the kitchen.

"You like your eggs scrambled hard or soft?" he called out.

She hadn't budged. "I hate eggs. And I told you I'm sick."

He popped his head out of the kitchen a minute later, waving the empty carton of ice cream in his hand. "Is this the culprit?"

Julie felt her face heat up.

Ben grinned broadly. "And you thought I wasn't much of an investigator."

She glowered at him. Ben, on the other hand, continued observing her with that grin plastered on his face.

"My guess is," he drawled laconically, "you don't know that, with the light streaming in from that window behind you, you can pretty much see through that demure cotton nightgown. Not that I'm complaining or anything . . ."

Julie's face went from pink to red. She grabbed her father's raincoat off the coatrack and threw it on. Then she stormed down the hall to the kitchen.

Ben was already at the fridge, pulling out the container of eggs.

"I told you I hate eggs," she snapped.

"You used to like eggs," he answered nonchalantly.

"How do you know what I used to like?" she demanded, clutching the oversize coat closed.

"You used to bring egg-salad sandwiches to school at least three times a week back in grade school."

"That was different. It was egg . . . salad. And anyway, I've changed. In case you haven't noticed. But then, I suppose since you haven't changed one iota, you probably think that the same goes for everyone you know. Or you're just too narcissistic to notice whether anyone else has done any growing up while you've remained frozen in time. And place," she added tartly.

He stopped cracking eggs into a glass bowl to turn and give her a considered survey.

"Will you stop it?" she demanded. She was becoming completely unnerved by his stare. By his presence. Hell, by his very existence.

"I'm just trying to see if you're right. If you have changed."

"Of course I've changed," she said irritably. "I'm nothing like . . . who I used to be."

Ben continued his unabashed study. "No."

Julie's forehead puckered. "What do you mean, no?"

"I mean I don't think you've changed all that much, Jules."

She put her hands on her hips. The insolence of the man. "Well, that just goes to show you how much you know."

"I'll tell you one thing I know," he said, setting down the hand eggbeater and starting across the room toward her. "I know that there are still the same sparks between us like there always were."

"Now you stop that this instant, Ben Sandler," she said fiercely as he started closing the gap between them again. "There are no sparks. There never were . . . no sparks."

"Any sparks," he corrected with a bad-boy smile.

Great. She couldn't even speak straight anymore. Even worse, think straight.

As Ben approached, she started to back up as she'd done the night before in the greenroom, but then she came to an abrupt stop. She refused to allow him to put her on the defensive. No, this time she would stand her ground. Besides, she was already backed up to the kitchen table.

She gave him a defiant look, determined to prove to Ben Sandler that he couldn't just go around snapping his fingers and having her fall into his arms, dying to be kissed, every time he was so inclined. She most definitely did not want to be kissed by him again, she told herself, as each of his steps brought him closer and closer. And her heart started racing faster and faster.

A bead of perspiration broke across her brow. She was sweltering in her father's lined raincoat. It must have been in the eighties in the kitchen.

"I don't know why you're doing this, Ben, but you're just wasting your time. I do not have the slightest romantic interest in you. I'm sorry if that hurts your feelings, or more likely your macho pride, but there it is. As far as that kiss last night . . . well, I wasn't exactly in my right mind. You could have been...anyone, and the same thing might have happened."

He smiled crookedly. "Even Captain Kangaroo?"

"Very funny." She did not, however, crack a smile herself.

He reached around her. An involuntary gasp escaped her lips. So much for her little speech. He leaned a bit closer. She was fast losing ground. And resolve.

Things seemed to be moving in slow motion. Damn, if he was going to kiss her again, why didn't he just get it over with?

Then, she heard the rustle of paper behind her. What the hell . . . ?

"Julie, I just had to tell you that you were fantastic last night. . . ."

"Oh, Ben, really. Cut the bull. . . ."

"'Right on, Julie. It's about time us women got our two cents in. . . .'"

Julie stared at Ben. *Us women?*

She twisted her head around. Ben was reading from a pink message slip he'd plucked from the mailbag, which was sitting on the table. She took the slip from his hand and shoved him out of the way. She finished reading the glowing praises of her debut performance on "Pittsville Patter."

In amazement, she read the end of the message out loud. "'Can't wait to see what you and Ben will spar about next week. We're with you all the way, Julie.'"

"I told you, Jules," Ben said softly as he watched her pluck another pink slip from the mailbag.

She read aloud, "'Tell Julie she hit the nail right on the head about the track and the minimall. The Punch and Julie Show was an added delight. Keep swinging. . . .'"

"I don't think she means that literally," Ben teased.

Julie grabbed another slip from the sack and ripped it open.

"'Boy, was I ever envious when Julie got to tangle with just about the sexiest man on television today. . . .'" Julie darted a look up at Ben. "To each his own," she muttered sardonically.

"Oh, and who's your pick, Jules?" he prodded. "Not that stuffed-shirt, supercilious jerk, Jordan Hammond?"

She almost came to Jordan's defense. Until she remembered that her feelings about her ex-anchor/ex-lover were even more negative than her feelings about Ben. Which was saying a lot.

"I could have told you that egotistical butt-kisser wasn't for you, Jules. You should count yourself lucky that he dumped you."

Julie's nostrils flared with indignation and fury. "Jordan Hammond did not dump me. We had a . . . mutual parting of the ways. On perfectly friendly terms." Okay, so she was stretching the truth a little. He had phoned her just before she left D.C. to tell her he didn't harbor any ill feelings about what she'd done to his jacket. Which was very big of him. His words, not hers!

"Have it any way you want it," Ben said blithely. "My point is, he was never the guy for you. No sparks, you know what I mean? No excitement. No heat."

"And how would you know that?" she retorted with more defensiveness than she would have liked.

"I watched the two of you on TV every week."

She gave him a dubious look.

"What?" he replied innocently. "You didn't know I was a big fan of yours?"

"No," she said succinctly. "And whether you ever watched the show or not, Ben Sandler, the point is that just because Jordan and I conducted ourselves with . . . with professional deportment on the air . . ."

"Professional deportment. I see. And tell me, Jules, how much fan mail did you get in D.C. about this 'professional deportment' going on between you and Hammond on the air?"

"The fan mail I received while I was on 'News and Views' had nothing to do with my relationship with Jordan. It had to do with issues, policies . . ."

"Congressional philanderers?"

"If you're referring to my pulling the covers on Senator Cooper, yes," she said with a defiant toss of her head.

"Pulling the covers, huh?" Ben said with a smile. "Good choice of words."

"Really, Ben, you are still the same impossible tease you were back in the second grade. You just love getting my goat. You love to see me make a fool of myself. Well, you must be damn proud of yourself," she said and, shoving him aside, she swept out of the room.

"Like the saying goes, Jules," Ben called after her, "if you can't stand the heat, get out of the kitchen."

After she left, Ben leaned against the counter, folded his arms across his chest and sighed. *What am I going to do about you, Jules? How am I going to prove to you that everything you want and need is right here in Pittsville?*

UP IN HER BEDROOM, Julie slammed the door and threw her father's raincoat down on the bed. Her nightgown clung to her damp skin. She peeled that off and angrily flung it aside.

She was standing in the middle of the room stark naked when there was a light rap on her door. A door that didn't have a lock on it. She snatched up the raincoat from the bed and held it up against her.

"Jules . . ." Ben said softly from the other side of the door.

"Don't you dare come in here, Ben. If you do . . . I will not be . . . accountable . . . for what may happen."

Ben smiled. "You're probably right about that, Jules," he said, his tone provocative and husky.

Julie's head was spinning. "Why are you doing this to me, Ben?"

"Don't you know?"

"I haven't got a clue."

She saw the doorknob turn. She rushed to stick the raincoat back on. "Ben, I'm warning you. . . ."

The door slowly opened. "Don't you want to know, Jules?"

He shut the door quietly behind him and ambled toward her.

"No," she said, feeling panicky. What was so disturbing was that her panic had less to do with the seductive glint in Ben's eyes than it did with the way her own pulse was racing and her stomach was knotting. And she couldn't blame it on the ice cream and taco chips. She quickly tried to blame it on sexual frustration. After all, it had been close to two months since she and Jordan . . .

Ben's words echoed uninvited in her mind. *No sparks. No excitement. No heat . . .* Wasn't that true, at least in part, off the air as well as on? But then, so what? A relationship was more than sparks, excitement, heat. At the moment, unfortunately, she couldn't think of what the "more" was. She was too busy feeling sparks, excitement, heat....

"I wasn't teasing you last night when I said I had a crush on you back in grade school, Jules. If you hadn't taken that swing at me, I'd have probably confessed I had the hots for you in high school, too."

"Oh, please."

"Right. Pretend you didn't know."

"I didn't know. I don't know. I don't believe you."

His gaze moved over her face with an intensity that unnerved her even more than his playful, irascible studies of her. "You scared the heck out of me in those days, Jules."

Surely he was kidding her. Only he looked dead serious. "I scared the heck out of you?"

"You were so sure of yourself. So sure you were going places...."

She was. She did.

Suddenly, she figured it out. Or thought she had. "I get it," she said.

Her shift in tone and expression took Ben by surprise. "You do?"

Her features hardened. "Back in high school I intimidated you because you saw me as someone who wasn't going to spend her life in a dead-end job in a two-bit town...."

"I wouldn't go so far as to say 'intimidated.'"

"But now you think I'm done for, all washed up. Now I'm down on my luck and you're the big man on campus. So now you can make a move, have that little fling you may actually have fantasized having with me back in high school. This is your way of getting back at me."

Ben folded his arms across his chest. His eyes narrowed. "I was wrong before. You *have* changed."

Julie was more taken aback by his hardened expression than by his words. "What's that supposed to mean?"

"You figure it out," he said, turning away.

She saw the fleeting look of hurt shadow his features, and impulsively she reached out to him. "Look, Ben. I'm sorry. I guess that was a little harsh."

He glanced back at her, his winsome expression making her breath catch in her throat.

"I always thought it was Samantha you had a crush on," she found herself saying in a half whisper.

"Samantha Warner?" He laughed. "Naw. She was too perfect."

"Gee, thanks a lot." And did he think Samantha Warner was "too perfect" in Paris? If she was so "perfect" why did he keep her picture on his desk?

A mischievous smile tilted the corner of Ben's mouth. "It was your imperfections that made you special, Jules."

"What imperfections?" she retorted. Okay, so she knew she wasn't perfect, but Ben's remark got to her.

He rubbed his thumb across his jaw thoughtfully. "Let's see. There's your smart-alecky mouth, your stubbornness, your impetuosity. Then there's that little scar over your right eyebrow—" Without warning, he gently drew his fingertips over the pencil-thin scar she'd got from falling off her bike when she was seven.

Hardly anyone ever noticed it, it was so faint. Leave it to Ben.

"The tiny chip in your front tooth . . . The way you used to stutter when you got excited . . ."

She pushed his hand away from her face; his touch provoked too many undesired flashes of arousal. "I did not stutter and I had that tooth capped years ago." She bared her teeth as proof.

Ben grinned. "Okay, so now you're almost perfect. I don't think we should let that stand in our way."

"We don't have a 'way,'" she insisted, although her statement definitely lacked conviction. That could be because her skin was still tingling from his brief touch.

"I still have a crush on you, Jules."

Again, ugly suspicions assaulted her. "Is this all about that fan mail downstairs . . . about talking me back into coanchoring 'Pittsville Patter' with you, Ben . . . ?"

"Do you really think that's what this is all about, Jules?"

"I don't know what this is all about, Ben. And that's the God's honest truth," she confessed, her voice a little shaky. "Please go home before I end up making a complete fool of myself again."

"Do you think this is any easier for me?" he asked softly. "For all I know, you're still crazy about that pompous ass of an anchor."

"He isn't . . . I'm not." Her mind was a complete jumble. "Will you listen to me? I can't even get out one coherent sentence. I'm coming unglued here, Ben. I ate a quart of ice cream last night. I ate a whole bag of taco chips. My mind and my body are turning to mush."

"Your body looks great," he murmured. "And I'm wild about your mind, Jules."

"This can't go anywhere. You know that, don't you?" Her voice was quaking now. "There's no future in this, for either one of us. I could be in Toledo this time next month. Or . . . Cleveland, Omaha . . ." The minute a decent spot came through for her she was off. Leaving Pittsville in the dust. Leaving Ben.

A bittersweet feeling swept over her. Ben did generate sparks in her; sparks she'd never felt with Jordan. Or with any other man, for that matter. Some of those sparks were downright incendiary. They could burn up all her energy and drive if she wasn't careful.

His hand moved to the lapel of her father's raincoat. "You don't really need this. It isn't raining in here."

Her gaze shot to the tossed nightgown on the floor. Ben's eyes followed. Then he focused back on her, the message clear that he knew she wasn't wearing anything under the coat.

He leaned forward, pressing his lips to her forehead, her nose, her cheek.

He was seducing her, plain and simple; tempting her despite everything she'd told him. He was banking on his sex appeal and charisma overcoming her resistance. An irresistible force meeting an implacable object. Only she wasn't feeling as implacable as she wished she was feeling.

She could see right through him. She knew exactly what he was doing. She just didn't seem able to do anything about it.

"This really is a bad idea, Ben," she said in a voice that was pathetically wishy-washy—something she'd never been, until now. She hated herself for it. She wanted to be firm, resolute. So why couldn't she make herself draw away from those tiny little kisses he was planting on her neck . . . ?

"I . . . I could name you a half-dozen reasons . . . why this isn't a good idea. . . ." She was nothing if not persistent, even in her worst moments. Unfortunately, so was Ben.

He tilted her head up and his mouth settled on hers, his incredible lips warm, inviting, lusty. Their tongues tangled. Only then did she realize just how starved she was for the taste and touch of him. If she'd admitted that to herself last night, she could have forgone the ice cream and taco chips, neither of which had offered her any comfort.

Ben nudged the oversize raincoat off her shoulders. The breeze fluttering in through her open window fanned her naked skin.

"Oh, Jules, you are so beautiful," he murmured, stepping back to take her all in. Then he moved closer again, his hands trailing down her body like she was a fine piece of sculpture and he was an artist relishing every one of her curves and textures. "Forget what I said before about imperfections," he whispered against her hair.

"Damn you, Ben," she said in a shaky voice, her pulse hammering. She feverishly attacked the buttons on his khaki shirt, her fingers trembling. What was she thinking? What was she doing? Then his mouth was on hers again and she couldn't think; couldn't stop.

And the kisses just got better and better. She practically ripped the shirt off his back, frantic to feel his skin against hers. As they clung to each other, kissing deeply, they were both working simultaneously on his jeans.

It was a toss-up who was trembling more, neither of them having quite expected this chain of events. Not that Ben hadn't been flooded with romantic images ever since he'd set eyes on her again. And last night, on the show, he'd literally felt like he'd come alive with Julie beside him. All the craziness on the set, her fury, the arguing, had done nothing to dissuade him from his longing for her. She'd been the girl of his dreams for so many years.

He stumbled, trying to step out of his jeans. They found themselves on the floor once again.

This time they both laughed—a moment of comic relief; long enough for Julie to regain a modicum of sanity. "Wait."

Ben stopped nibbling at her ear. "What?"

"Samantha."

"What?"

"Exactly. What about her?"

"Jules . . ."

"I know about Paris, Ben. I know about that photo on your desk."

"Nothing happened in Paris, Jules. Not between me and Samantha, anyway. I confess there was this very pretty French gal," he teased.

"So why the picture?" she persisted.

"It's a great shot of the Eiffel Tower."

"Right. And next you'll be trying to sell me the Brooklyn Bridge."

"Selling you a bridge is definitely not what I have in mind," he murmured, his gaze trailing down her luscious naked body, all the way down those chorus-girl legs to the tips of her toes. He was so aroused he couldn't think straight. And certainly, the last thing on his mind was Samantha Warner.

"Just tell me the truth, Ben."

"Okay, okay." He rolled off her, staring up at the ceiling, trying to get his breathing under control. "The truth is, perfect strangers stop by my office every now and then, and sort of . . . throw themselves at me. Or some sweet little granny drops by, wanting to fix me up with her granddaughter, or—"

"I get the message," Julie said dryly. "Women lust after you."

Ben grinned. "I guess you could put it that way." He turned on his side to face her, his fingers raking through her hair.

His touch sent a wave of desire curling through her. "And the picture?" she asked weakly.

"I point to it, sigh, and say I'm really not ready for another relationship yet," he said dramatically. "They nod winsomely and amble out of my office and that's the whole story. Samantha means nothing to me, Jules. Never did."

"Really?"

"Really," he whispered as his head descended.

Julie cried out as his mouth closed over her nipple.

It wasn't, however, from excitement. It was from horror, as she stared toward the now open door of her bedroom where Kate and Rachel were standing in shocked silence, their mouths gaping open.

*"Oops,"* Rachel muttered.

# 4

KATE AND RACHEL WERE sitting around the table in their father's kitchen when Julie entered, Ben having made a hasty exit out the front door. She was fully dressed now in a pair of cutoffs and an old Pittsville Panthers T-shirt she'd grabbed out of a bureau drawer.

"Wow, these comments are something," Rachel said with forced brightness as she plucked one message out of the sack and started reading it as if Julie weren't even there.

"We're getting calls from all over the area from people wanting to be on the show," Kate said, glancing over at Julie but quickly settling her gaze on Rachel. "It's ironic. I thought after the bashing Rockman got, everyone would be scared to come on. Instead, I've got more takers than I can book for the next three months."

"And the calls from potential sponsors have been amazing," Rachel added, avoiding eye contact with Julie altogether. "Totally amazing."

Julie stood just inside the kitchen door listening to her sisters prattle on. Finally, hands on her hips, she said, "Isn't anyone going to say anything?"

Both sisters looked at her. Of course they had been talking, but they knew precisely what Julie meant.

"I guess . . . we should have . . . knocked," Rachel mumbled.

"Right," Kate hurriedly added.

Silence followed. What else was there to say?

Julie crossed the room and slumped into a chair. "Coffee. I need a cup of coffee."

Rachel and Kate both sprang up at the same time. "I make better coffee than you do," Kate told her kid sister.

"I know," Rachel said enthusiastically. "I'll make some toast." She spotted the eggs still sitting out on the counter, a couple of them already cracked into a mixing bowl. "And eggs . . ."

"No eggs," Julie said so sharply, Kate and Rachel eyed each other nervously.

"Fine, Julie. No eggs, just toast," Rachel soothed, hastily sticking the eggs back in the refrigerator and then tending to the toast.

Kate, who was scooping coffee into the filter, added a couple of extra scoops, figuring Julie would need it good and strong.

Julie sat still, feeling numb and dazed. "I should probably thank you both," she muttered.

"Thank us for what?" Kate said. "Embarrassing the whole lot of us?"

"No," Julie replied with a vigorous shake of her head that sent her blond hair flying all over her face. "For saving me from making a major mistake. Talk about a close call. If you'd arrived a few minutes later . . . Well, anyway . . ." She wiped a line of perspiration from her brow. "It is so hot in here."

Rachel quickly fanned herself with her hand. "Mmm. Yes. Hot. It is hot."

"Some of us are hotter than others of us," Kate said, regaining her dry wit.

Julie darted her a look. "Okay, I lost my head. That is, I *almost* lost my head. It's just that Ben is so . . ." She stopped. No, it wasn't fair to blame it on him. Sure, he'd seduced her; but she'd been anything but an innocent bystander. He hadn't duped her. She was a willing—hell, an active—participant.

"A lot of women find him irresistible," Rachel said, grabbing the popped bread from the toaster.

"Well, I for one am going to resist him from now on. The last thing I need right now is a . . . a fling. Especially with a man I've known and been at war with practically my whole life."

"It looked to me like you were calling a truce up there," Kate said glibly. "Or was it hand-to-hand combat?"

Rachel couldn't help laughing. "I didn't really see any hands."

Julie slapped her hand down on the table. "Go on, you two. Make jokes while my personal and professional life is going down the tubes."

Kate poured a steaming mug of coffee for Julie and brought it over to her. "Skipping your personal life for a moment," she said, sitting down beside her, "your debut on 'Pittsville Patter' was a star turn. I know we're just a hokey little station, but word is out all over the county that this is the show to watch. If you want my advice—"

"I don't," Julie said succinctly.

"I think you should go over the set changes I drew up last night, sit down with Ben and pick out your guests for the next couple of months. Well, we've already got next week's guest scheduled in, but after that—"

"A couple of months? No way. I was going to do it for a month . . . tops."

"Okay, for the next month," Kate said.

Rachel brought over the toast. "Really, Julie, what do you have to lose? And just think about how much you'd be doing for WPIT. For Kate. We could double, triple the cost of airtime for the show and we'd still have sponsors beating down our doors."

Julie looked from Rachel to Kate. "It doesn't make any sense. I made a complete fool of myself on the show. Not to mention I drove our guest off ten minutes before the show ended."

"Good thing, too," Kate said. "At least ninety percent of the callers thought the last segment was the best part of the show. We're going to make it a regular feature."

"Oh, absolutely," Rachel enthused. "You and Ben can debate a different issue each week."

"It can be anything from local politics and world events to movies, books, relationships—"

"Relationships? Oh, no," Julie said firmly.

"Okay, fine. You and Ben work it out," Kate said.

"I don't think it even matters what the two of you discuss," Rachel said. "It's the chemistry—"

Kate nudged Rachel.

"What I mean is," Rachel said quickly, "it's the dynamic interplay, the energy, the . . ." She looked over to Kate for help.

"The antipathy," Kate offered dryly.

"Right," Rachel said. "The antipathy."

Julie laughed harshly. "Where was that antipathy when I really needed it?"

"I WANT YOU TO KNOW," Julie said to Kate the next day as they sifted through a furniture catalog in Kate's office, "that the main reason I'm going along with this show is to do my bit for WPIT."

"And I appreciate it," Kate said.

"And also because, after Jordan, I vowed never again to get personally involved with my coanchor. So, as long as Ben and I are working together, I can make it adamantly clear to him that anything...personal is off-limits. It simply complicates matters too much and I feel it doesn't allow me to be as effective and uninhibited...."

"Uninhibited. Right."

"On the air. I'm talking about being uninhibited on the show," Julie clarified.

"Fine," Kate said, tapping a picture of a round oak table. "What do you think of this?"

Julie looked down at the catalog. "It looks like it belongs in a dining room."

Kate grinned. "That's because it's a dining-room table."

Julie turned several pages, but she was having trouble concentrating on what was on any of them. "Let's face it. We've got nothing in common. There's not one single thing we both agree on. And he doesn't take anything seriously."

"I don't know," Kate deadpanned. "He looked pretty serious up there in your bedroom."

Julie picked up the catalog and bopped it over her sister's head.

"Sorry," Kate said, grinning. "I couldn't resist."

A smile tugged at the corners of Julie's mouth. "Yeah. Neither could I. That was the problem."

They both broke into laughter.

"Care to let me in on the joke?" Ben inquired, popping his head into the office.

Julie shot Kate a look. "No."

"Okay, okay. I won't pry," Ben said. "I'm just happy to see you laughing for a change, Jules."

"I happen to laugh plenty," Julie retorted.

Ben strolled into the office with his typical languid grace. "About what? No, really, Jules. I honestly want to know what tickles your funny bone."

"I can tell you plenty of things that don't," she said tightly.

Kate rose from her chair. "Listen, if you two are going to go at it again—" She stopped abruptly, realizing the double entendre—and seeing that the two of them realized it, too. She scurried around the desk and headed quickly for the door. "I've got to see Meg. She's got this new corn ice cream she wants me to sample before her show this afternoon. Corn ice cream. Can you imagine? What will Meg think of next?"

Kate was out the door before she could get a response.

Ben grinned at Julie. "Corn ice cream. Bet you couldn't down a gallon of that flavor."

"It wasn't a gallon. It was a quart. And it was half empty."

"I'm only teasing, Jules." He regarded her with a disconcerting mix of amusement and desire.

"That's the trouble."

He shoved his hands into the pockets of his jeans. "Okay, let's be serious."

"No. That's even more trouble," she admitted.

They both smiled. Neither of them said anything for a long minute. Their smiles faded.

"So, where does it leave us, Jules?" he asked quietly.

She tapped the open page in the catalog on Kate's desk. "Tell me what you think of this table for the set." Her voice sounded husky because her throat was dry. She couldn't quite meet his eyes because for some reason they made her ache inside.

He came over to the desk and stood so close to her, she could hear him exhale. Their shoulders brushed. She meant to move away, but her feet didn't seem to be able to budge.

"Which one?" His question whispered by her ear.

She swallowed hard, pointing to the same one her sister had pointed out to her. "This one."

He leaned closer, his breath fanning her face. "Hmm. Nice."

"Fine. Then we'll order it. With six matching captain's chairs." She slapped the catalog closed. They were still shoulder to shoulder.

"You really should get a lock for your bedroom door, Jules."

She turned to face him and had to suck in her breath to proceed. "I won't need a lock, Ben. What happened this morning . . . What almost happened . . . isn't going to almost happen again."

"Well, at least you didn't say it could have happened with anyone. Even Captain Kangaroo."

"See, that's what I mean. You don't take anything seriously."

"You're wrong, Jules. I take what's happening between us very seriously."

Their eyes met and held. "Well, you shouldn't," she muttered, pulling her gaze away.

He smiled ruefully. "You've got to make up your mind, Jules. First you accuse me of not taking things seriously, then you tell me I'm taking things too seriously. I think we're going around in circles, here. I know my head's spinning. How's your's doing?" He reached out and lifted her chin, forcing her eyes to confront his again.

"Not too well," she confessed.

"Jules . . ." He tried to draw her into his arms. For a moment, she felt herself weaken, but then she pulled away. "Look, Ben, I know it's a cliché, but I just don't think we should mix business with . . . anything other than business."

Ben felt a flash of irritation. "Is that what you told Jordan Hammond?"

"No. That's what I learned from my experience with Jordan Hammond," she said tartly. "Now, shall we go over who the guest is going to be for our next show?"

EVERYONE IN THE Full Moon Café greeted Delaney Parker warmly as he walked in for his usual three o'clock break from the station house. Betty, a fixture in the place, started cutting him a slab of freshly made apple pie the minute he walked in. By the time he got to the counter, the pie and a steaming mug of black coffee were waiting for him.

"How's the father-to-be holding up?" Betty asked. "I saw Rachel yesterday and if she doesn't just glow, I don't know what you'd call it."

"She not only glows," Delaney said, "she's calm as a cucumber. I'm the one that's a nervous wreck. The other day I bought her a new overnight case for the hospital and I wanted her to pack it up so she'd be ready."

Betty chuckled.

"Yeah, Rachel laughed, too," Delaney said, catching sight of Ben Sandler sitting alone in one of the booths.

Betty sighed. "I suppose you saw his show the other night. You'd think the guy would be walking on cloud nine the way everyone in the whole region is raving. Why, Rachel told me that she's got more sponsors for the show than she knows what to do with."

Delaney grabbed up his mug and pie plate. "Think I'll go over and see if I can cheer him up."

When Delaney slid into the bench seat across from Ben, the anchorman didn't even acknowledge him.

Delaney sipped on his coffee, munched a bite of pie.

Ben was nursing a lemonade. An untouched glazed doughnut sat on his plate. Without looking across at Delaney, he muttered, "What gives with them, Parker?"

"The Hart girls in general? Or Julie Hart in particular?"

"Now, you take Rachel."

"I did take her," Delaney said with a smile.

"Exactly. And did she fight you tooth and nail from start to finish?"

"Well, we did have our rocky moments," Delaney replied.

Ben wasn't listening. "No. I blame that creep, Hammond. I think he soured Jules on men." He took a sip of his lemonade. "And Kate's not much of a help. She's so down on men herself, some of it was bound to rub off on Jules."

"Julie impresses me as a woman with a very strong mind of her own," Delaney said, after swallowing down another bite of pie. "I don't think she's easily influenced by anyone."

Ben picked up his doughnut, but instead of biting into it he waved it at Delaney. "You're right. She's stubborn."

Ben set the doughnut down, changing his mind. "No. She's scared. And something else I've discovered about her. She loves putting other people on the spot, but try to put her there and she's ducking for cover faster than a stealth bomber." He rolled his eyes. "Stealth bombers. That's the issue she wants to debate on our next show."

"Sounds . . . interesting."

Ben grinned. "What's going to be interesting is how she's going to segue into stealth bombers after the guest in our first segment."

"Oh? Who's the guest?"

Ben's grin widened, his eyes sparkling mischievously. "Dr. Marion Kendell. A sex therapist."

Delaney laughed. "Now that's a show I won't want to miss."

"WE SPEND SO MUCH TIME fighting about sex and love. In my opinion," Dr. Marion Kendell said dramatically, "we would all be a lot better off fighting *for* sex and love. You know what I mean?"

Ben grinned at the diminutive fifty-something sex therapist whose feet didn't quite touch the floor as she sat on the couch with her ankles crossed—the new furniture for the set hadn't yet arrived; nor was the new backdrop ready.

"I couldn't agree more, Dr. Kendell," Ben said enthusiastically, then turned to Julie who sat tight-lipped in her chair.

"Sex and love don't always go together," Julie said archly. "One's a purely physical drive while the other's . . . more emotional, ephemeral . . . elusive."

"Ah, that's very true, Julie," Dr. Kendell said with a smile. "The true joy is when the two go hand in hand."

To Julie's horror, Ben chose that precise moment to reach out and squeeze her hand. She quickly pulled it away, turning beet red as she caught the sex therapist's knowing smile. How many out there in television land were also busy putting two and two together and coming up with the wrong answer? Or what Julie was determined was going to be the "wrong answer" from now on.

She shivered inwardly. Her personal relationship with Ben—or what everyone would be surmising was their personal relationship—could turn into a local media event. This was all she needed. Trying to remain professional and poised with Ben as her coanchor was proving all but impossible.

"Sex and love. A winning combination," Ben was saying with great enthusiasm. "Tell me something, Dr. Kendell. When a man and a woman really click . . . You know what I'm saying—when sparks fly, passions soar, hearts race . . . ?"

Dr. Kendell smiled. "I think I get the picture, Ben."

So did Julie, the camera crew, everyone else in the studio, and probably everyone watching the show. Last week Julie had been mortified when her chair had given way and sent her hurtling to the ground. Now she only wished something like that would happen—anything to divert attention away from Ben's "discussion about sex and love" with Dr. Kendell.

"Well," Ben went on earnestly, "wouldn't you say that something like that happens very rarely, and when it does . . . ?" Ben paused, struggling for the right way to phrase it.

Dr. Kendell beat him to the punch. "Are you trying to say you shouldn't look a gift horse in the mouth?"

Ben waved his index finger in the air. "Exactly. Don't you agree, Dr. Kendell? After all, you're the expert here."

"I certainly do think when two adult, responsible people feel mutual passion and desire and there's nothing standing in their way—" Dr. Kendell began to expound.

"Aha," Julie cut in. "Isn't it true that there is often something standing in their way? Lust alone does not a relationship make," she said pompously.

Ben smirked.

Dr. Kendell gave her a bemused look.

"What about . . . incompatibility?" Julie demanded defensively.

"What about opposites attracting?" Ben countered, before Dr. Kendell could respond.

"What about careers? Sometimes a woman—or a man—has to put career over . . . other interests," Julie argued. "Naturally," she added, "I'm speaking for many of the women and men who are watching our show. People who've worked very hard to get someplace. Or who are currently working toward a . . . a particular career goal. These people have to be very . . . directed, determined, unswayed by what might only turn out to be . . ."

"A passing fancy?" Dr. Kendell suggested.

Julie could feel the heat rising up her neck. "Well . . . yes."

"Sure, if you've got one foot in the door and one foot out, it'll pass," Ben said sardonically. "You've got to stay around long enough to tell whether a relationship has any future in it. Aren't I right, Dr. Kendell?"

"Well, naturally a relationship takes time," the good doctor began.

"Not everyone has the time," Julie retorted heatedly.

"Isn't it important to make time, Dr. Kendell?" Ben demanded. "Let's face it. You can't cuddle up with your career at night. Your career won't stroke your body and tell you how desirable you are. Careers come and go—"

"And love doesn't?" Julie blurted out, Jordan Hammond having shot into her mind.

Ben turned to her. "Not if it's the real thing."

Julie sneered at him. "The real thing. You sound like you're pitching soda pop. Anyway, who's to say when it's the 'real thing,' as you put it?"

"You feel it. Right here," Ben said, thumping his chest.

"That's romantic nonsense," Julie said derisively.

"That's not quite—" Dr. Kendell started to say, only for Ben to cut her off.

He eyeballed Julie. "Some people are just afraid to listen to their hearts."

Julie arched a brow. "Some people are just afraid to think with their heads."

"Some people think too much."

"Some people don't think at all."

"In my view," Dr. Kendell began, trying again to get a word in edgewise. No chance. Both Julie and Ben had forgotten all about her.

"It's the chase, that's what it is. They always want you till they've got you. It all boils down to male ego," Julie said with unmasked cynicism. "Then once they have you, they get bored or you do something they don't approve of and they dump you."

"Aha," Ben said.

"Aha what?" Julie demanded.

Ben smiled crookedly. "So he did dump you."

Julie turned scarlet. "I was not talking *personally,*" she said through clenched teeth.

"Sure you weren't," Ben deadpanned.

"You think you know so much," Julie snapped, forgetting not only about their guest, but the cameras, the viewers out there in television land. She sat poised on the edge of her seat. "Well, you're wrong. There's plenty you don't know. . . ."

Ben also moved to the edge of his seat. His knees touched Julie's knees. "There's plenty I do know. I know that people have to take chances. They have to trust love, accept it instead of running scared."

"Who's running scared? If there's anyone who's scared . . ."

"Connecting is what it's all about. Marriage, kids . . ."

"Next you'll tell me a house with a picket fence, a mutt."

Ben grinned. "A house with a picket fence. A mutt, a cat, maybe even a parakeet."

"Well, some women want more than that, Ben."

"Really? And what is it 'some women' want, Jules?"

"Self-fulfillment. A sense of accomplishment. A feeling of having succeeded at something you've strived for all your life." She took in a breath. "And don't call me Jules."

"It happens to be a term of endearment."

"I don't happen to want to be referred to by a 'term of endearment,'" she hissed.

"What *do* you want?" Ben's voice was rife with frustration.

"What do I want? What do I want? I'll tell you what I want—"

"Excuse me—" Dr. Kendell finally managed to break in "—but that man over there keeps waving at you."

"What?" the twosome said irritably in unison. Then they both caught sight of Gus signaling a station break.

Ben grinned into camera one. "We've got to go to a commercial, folks. Stay tuned."

"Oh my God," Julie gasped, the instant they were off the air. "I did it again," she muttered, mortified. "I can't believe I let myself go like that."

She glared at Ben. "This is all your fault."

"My fault?" Ben said innocently. "Seems to me you were the one—"

"Oh, shut up," Julie said, close to tears. She shut her eyes. "That was awful."

Dr. Kendell was removing her mike. She smiled saucily. "Oh no, Julie. I thought it was very... stimulating. All that energy, that fire . . . that passion. I'm only sorry my husband's out of town tonight," she said with a little sigh.

*August 5*

Well, this time Aunt Julie didn't lock herself in the greenroom after the show, she just stormed out of the studio, flew into her car, and burned rubber as she drove off into the night. Ben went racing after her, but he stopped for a second when he passed me in the hall. "Isn't she something?" he said, with this big smile on his face.

"I think she's pretty pissed off," I said, then got worried mom was in earshot. She hates when I say things like "pissed off." Lucky for me, she was still in the control room with Aunt Rachel and the others.

Ben pinched my cheek—I really hate it when people do that, but when Ben did it, well, he didn't do it like most people do, so I didn't mind all that much.

"She's just mad," he said in this real cheery voice, "because we never did get to debate stealth bombers in our last segment."

Stealth bombers? Bo-rrring! I, for one, am glad Aunt Julie and Ben picked up right where they left off for their last segment. They spent the whole last ten minutes arguing over things like men always wanting to be in control and confusing lust with love and stuff like that. I guess a year ago, maybe even a few months ago, I would have thought all that kind of "mushy" talk was totally stupid. Now, I find it kind of interesting. At least, the way Aunt Julie and Ben "talk" about it.

Delaney said it was a wonder Aunt Julie didn't end up socking Ben in the jaw again during the show. Mom said she should have. Aunt Rachel said she was never again going to walk in on Aunt Julie without knocking.

I wonder what Aunt Rachel meant by that? Grown-ups. You just can't figure them....

# 5

"I CAN'T BELIEVE IT," Julie said incredulously.

Kate grinned. "Believe it."

Two bright pink spots blossomed on Julie's cheeks. "This is just about the most insulting—"

"Oh, come on, Julie," Kate cut her off with a laugh. "Where's your sense of humor?"

There was no sign of it on Julie's face. She sat across from Kate in her sister's office at WPIT looking totally dejected. "I'm supposed to laugh because some television writer thinks 'Pittsville Patter' would make a great sitcom? And he thinks I'd be great in the lead? I knew I was laughable as an anchor. I guess this proves it."

Kate continued to smile as she picked up another letter from a huge stack of mail. "Here," she said. "Maybe this one will make you feel bette1

Julie looked over at the sheet of notepaper in her sister's hand. She hesitated. "If this is another example of your own warped sense of humor, Kate, I really can't . . ."

"Will you just read it?" Kate persisted.

Julie took tentative hold of the sheet, her eye catching the masthead first. *"Happening?"* She looked warily across at her sister. *Happening* was the newest and hottest entertainment magazine on the market. "Why would . . . ?"

"For goodness' sake, Julie, read the damn letter," Kate said, exasperated.

Julie read in stunned silence. Then she reread it, again without saying a word. Her eyes were still glued to the paper when Kate said impatiently, "Well?"

Julie had to tear her eyes away from the sheet. "I don't believe it."

"Small world, huh? To think that Ron Jamison, the publisher of the hottest rag in town, would have a summer house right here in the Berkshires and would have, just by chance, caught this week's episode of 'Pittsville Patter.'" Kate leaned across the desk, tapping the letter. "What did Jamison say about the show?" As if Kate didn't know. As if she hadn't memorized the whole letter.

Julie stared at the letter again, but she didn't say anything.

Kate quoted. "'A battle of wits that was tart, funny, sexy, tremendously entertaining.' And then, didn't he compare you and Ben to Hepburn and Tracy?"

Julie continued to sit there, dazed. Not only did Ron Jamison rave about the show, and especially about her and Ben as coanchors, he wanted to fly in one of the magazine's top reporters from Manhattan to do a feature story on them.

Kate saw the frown start to develop on her sister's face. "What's the matter? Isn't this just the kind of break you've been hoping for? National media attention? A chance to get back in the public eye?"

"That's what I'm afraid of," Julie replied. "What if this reporter writes a piece that makes me look like a complete fool? How's that going to win me favor as a serious anchor with any of the networks?"

"'Tart, funny, sexy, tremendously entertaining.' That's not how Jamison would describe a fool," Kate argued. "A feature story," she reiterated. "Come on, Julie. You should be leaping around this office doing cartwheels."

Julie broke into a smile. "I haven't done a cartwheel in years. Not since high school."

"Are you telling me you can't do them anymore?" Kate challenged, biting back a grin.

"Of course, I could. I'm in better shape now— Well, maybe not better, but I'm still . . . pretty limber. . . ."

"Prove it."

Julie stared at her sister. "Are you serious? You really want me to do a cartwheel right here in your office? Now?"

Kate nonchalantly shrugged her shoulders. "Not if you don't think . . ."

Julie's eyes flashed. She never could resist a challenge. Popping up from her seat, she kicked off her pumps, hiked her short, straight, black linen skirt way up her thighs, and did a couple of deep knee bends as a warm-up. Meanwhile, Kate also sprang up and shoved a cluttered coffee table closer to her office couch so that Julie would have enough space in the middle of the room to make her acrobatic move.

Kate glanced at Julie. "You're sure you can still . . ."

"Oh, shut up," Julie said, raising her arms up over her head, the tails of her white silk shirt coming undone from her waistband.

She was mid-flight when Kate's door opened and Ben appeared.

"Argh!" Julie gasped as she caught sight of him just as she was making what would have been an expert landing, had she not been "distracted"!

As Julie crashed to a heap on the floor, a loud grunt escaping her lips, Ben and Kate both rushed to her aid.

"Don't touch me," Julie snapped as Ben reached for her. She struggled to tug her skirt back down, but winced in pain.

"Oh, Julie, have you broken something?" Kate asked anxiously, feeling horribly guilty for goading her sister into doing such a dumb stunt.

"No," Julie said tightly, her eyes narrowing on Ben. "But I know something I'd like to break."

Ben looked affronted. "What? You're going to blame this on me, too?"

"Don't you ever knock before you barge into a room?" she demanded.

Ben's eyes shot to Kate, an impish smile on his lips. "I guess I should have, but I'm not the only one who forgets to knock." Kate blushed and guiltily averted her eyes.

He returned his gaze to Julie. "Anyway, I didn't barge in. I had a memo waiting on my desk from Kate saying to come see her the minute I got here." He tried to look contrite, but he didn't pull it off very well.

"That's true," Kate admitted.

Julie was still sitting on the floor. She tried to rise, only to wince again as she started to put pressure on her right foot.

"You *are* hurt," Kate said anxiously.

"It's nothing," Julie insisted, managing—with considerable pain, which she valiantly tried to hide—to get to her feet. Then she hobbled, with Kate's assistance, over to the couch. "Just my ankle. I probably twisted it a little." She sank down on the couch, a bead of perspiration glistening above her upper lip.

Ben knelt down and examined her ankle. "It's starting to swell." He poked it gently.

"Ouch!" Julie exclaimed. "I thought I told you not to touch me."

"It could be broken," Ben said to Kate, ignoring Julie.

"It isn't broken," Julie declared.

"You're right," Kate said.

"There," Julie said contemptuously to Ben. "Kate agrees."

"No," Kate countered. "Actually, I was agreeing with Ben. You need to get an X ray, Julie. For workmen's compensation."

"Oh, please. I'm telling you, it's nothing. I just need a little ice—"

Before she knew what was happening, Ben had scooped her up in his arms.

"What do you think you're doing, Ben Sandler?" Julie cried out indignantly.

"I'm taking you over to the medical center to get that ankle X-rayed," he said calmly. "And you can tell me why you were playing gymnast while I drive you over there."

"I do not need to be carried out of here. Just put me down. Kate can help me. . . ."

Ben hiked her up a little higher in his arms. "Will you do me a big favor, Jules?"

"What?" she asked sullenly.

"Shut up," he said with a grin. He glanced back at Kate as he headed out the door with Julie squirming in his arms. "About that memo . . ."

Kate grinned. "It's connected to the cartwheel. Julie can tell you all about it."

Julie glared at her sister as she was being carried off. "I may never talk to either one of you ever again."

"I TOLD YOU IT WASN'T broken," Julie said smugly as she hobbled on crutches out of the medical center, her nevertheless badly sprained ankle taped up with an Ace bandage. Per doctor's orders, she was to keep off the ankle for a couple of weeks.

Ben smiled complacently. "I can't be one hundred percent right all the time, Jules."

"Ha!"

They got to the steps outside the building. "We can use the ramp," Ben suggested as he saw Julie hesitate.

"That won't be necessary," she said archly.

She actually did fine on the first two steps. It was when she got to the third step that it turned into a disaster in the making. The tip of one of her crutches slipped from the step below just as she was swinging herself down to it. Her mouth opened in a silent scream as she saw first her crutch go flying down the steps to the ground below, knowing that she was about to go flying after it. . . .

Ben caught her in his arms in the nick of time. For once she didn't utter a peep of protest; just clung to him.

Ben was a bit shaken himself. Still, he managed to make the most of having Julie in his arms once again.

It took a couple of seconds for her to realize that everyone passing in and out of the medical center was taking avid note of their embrace. No doubt, many were viewers of "Pittsville Patter." Then a car passed by, the driver tooting at them, his hand held high out the window with a thumbs-up sign. Several more drivers followed suit.

*Just what I was afraid of,* Julie thought despondently. *We are becoming a local media event.* She desperately wanted to push away from Ben at this point, but it was easier said than done, given that she was now minus one of her crutches and she couldn't put any weight on her right foot. Like it or not, she needed Ben's assistance to make it down the rest of the steps.

"The gossip's going to be flying now," she muttered grumpily. "Will you please just help me get to your car and take me home?"

Ben supported her with his arm around her waist until they made it to the sidewalk. Then he bent and retrieved her crutch.

She snatched it from him and fit it under her arm, leading the way to his car, which was parked in the lot at the side of the medical center.

Once she was settled in the passenger seat, her crutches laid out in the back, Ben got behind the wheel and pulled out.

"You still haven't told me why you were doing a cartwheel in Kate's office," Ben said, glancing over at her, "and what it has to do with Kate's memo about wanting to see me on the double."

"As for the cartwheel, that was Kate's doing. She dared me."

Ben smiled.

"I would have done just fine, if you hadn't burst in. I could have done it one-handed. No-handed."

"I don't doubt it," Ben said, his smile deepening.

Julie began to shake her head. "I don't know what's come over me lately."

Ben slipped her a look. "Don't you?"

Julie looked away. What with her ankle throbbing and her heart still pounding from that near fall down the steps—or was it pounding from Ben's embrace on the steps?—she was feeling particularly vulnerable, and wanted to steer clear of the topic Ben was trying to lead her into.

"Have you ever heard of *Happening*? The entertainment magazine?"

"I live in Pittsville, not on the planet Mars, Jules. Sure, I've heard of *Happening*. I read it in the dentist's waiting room all the time."

"Bad teeth?" Julie asked sardonically.

He bared a shiny white-toothed smile. "What do you think?"

Okay, so he could do toothpaste commercials. "It seems Ron Jamison, the publisher of *Happening*, caught our last show."

"Really?" Ben said.

It wasn't what he said but how he said it that made Julie give him a curious look. "You don't sound all that surprised."

Ben shrugged. "Well, I wasn't sure . . ."

"Wasn't sure of what?"

Ben came to a stop at a red light. He glanced over at her. "Wasn't sure he'd watch it."

Julie gave him a dubious look. "Wait a second. Are you trying to tell me you had something to do with Jamison watching the show?"

"If by 'something' you mean did I give him a buzz and suggest he catch it, I guess the answer is yes," Ben said blithely, slipping into first and pulling out as the light turned green.

"You're telling me you phoned Ron Jamison, a perfect stranger..."

"No."

"No, you didn't phone Jamison?"

"No," Ben said, turning left onto Julie's street. "He's not a perfect stranger."

"You *know* Ron Jamison, the publisher of *Happening?*"

"Well, I wouldn't say we were best friends...."

"What would you say?" Julie demanded as he pulled up at the curb in front of her father's gray-shingled Victorian house.

Ben shut off the engine and started to open his door.

"Where are you going?"

"Sit tight," Ben said, exiting the car and shutting his door behind him. He came around and opened her door as she struggled to reach for her crutches in the back seat. Before she'd retrieved them, she once again found herself being scooped up into Ben's arms.

"I can manage perfectly well—" she started to protest. "Just put me down, give me my crutches and you can go back to work."

"Don't you want to hear about me and Ron?"

AFTER BEN SETTLED Julie on the couch in the living room, he went off to the kitchen to make her a cup of tea even though she'd made it very clear she did not want a cup of tea.

"Fine," he told her. He'd make himself a cup.

She hobbled into the kitchen on her crutches. "Okay, so how do you know Jamison?"

"I thought I told you to sit tight."

"I don't like being ordered about," she said tartly.

Ben grinned. He filled the teakettle, turned off the tap and set the kettle on the stove.

"So?" Julie demanded impatiently.

"Will you please sit down?"

She started to protest.

"That wasn't an order, Jules. I said 'please.'"

Grousing, she reluctantly crossed over to a chair at the kitchen table, and eased herself down to it. More because her ankle ached than because of Ben's "request."

Ben leaned against the counter, nodding his approval.

Impatiently she flung back a fallen lock of blond hair. "Come on, Ben..."

"He was looking for a getaway place and he ended up buying the old Scott place down on Simon Pond Road."

Julie stared at him. "You mean he's your neighbor? Ron Jamison actually bought the house next door to you?" Simon Pond Road was one block long. There were only two properties on it. The old Scott farm and Ben's cottage, which had, at one time, been part of the Scott property.

"Great guy," Ben said. "And the sweetest wife and kiddies. Taught Martin, that's the oldest one, how to fly fish down at their creek last summer. And Lauren—" He stopped, pressing his fingers to his lips and then flinging his hand into the air in an exuberant gesture. "She makes an apple pie that would put Meg Cromwell's version to shame." He grinned broadly. "Admittedly, not that that would be hard to do."

"Lauren? Another of Ron's kiddies?"

"Ron's wife. The sweetest woman..."

"You said that already."

"She used to be a reporter herself—that's how she and Ron met—but she decided to give up her career to raise a family."

Julie groaned audibly.

"Your ankle?" Ben asked solicitously, knowing full well that wasn't the reason for the groan.

"To each his own," Julie said derisively.

The water started to boil. Ben made two cups of tea and brought them to the table. "They've done wonders with the place," he said. "They even put up a picket fence around the property. Painted it white."

Julie forgot she'd told Ben she didn't want the tea and absently took a sip. "And—don't tell me—they've got a mutt, a cat, a parakeet—"

"Two mutts."

"I should have guessed."

"They're terrific."

"The mutts?"

Ben grinned. "The Jamisons."

"So, you know about the feature story he wants to do."

Ben shook his head. "All I did was suggest he catch the show while he was out here. So he wants to do a feature story? On us?"

"He wants to send a reporter out here from Manhattan this weekend." Julie hesitated. "It seems he thinks we're . . . Hepburn and Tracy reincarnated."

Ben smiled provocatively. "Hepburn and Tracy. Weren't those two madly in love?"

"Could we please discuss this impending interview, Ben?"

"Sure," he said pleasantly, taking the chair next to her. "What do you want to discuss?"

Julie shifted uncomfortably in her seat. "Ben, this story could either be a boost to my fast-declining career or it could be the final nail in my coffin." She leveled her gaze at him. "And since I know how you feel . . ."

Ben pulled his chair closer to her, meeting her gaze. "You're afraid I'm going to screw things up for you?"

Julie sighed. "It's one thing to be made a laughingstock on a little local show that maybe a few thousand people at most tune in to." She paused. "Millions of people read *Happening,* Ben."

Ben kept staring at her, not saying a word. The silence dragged on.

"It's just that—"

He held up his hand to silence her. "You don't have to worry, Julie," he said finally.

*Julie?* Surely this was the first time since she'd returned to Pittsville that he hadn't called her "Jules." Come to think of it, she couldn't remember a time when he hadn't called her Jules. For all her complaints about his using that "endearment," not hearing him use it now was oddly jarring.

He rose from his seat. "I won't screw it up for you," he said curtly.

He started to walk away from the table, his expression unnervingly distant.

Julie was a little shaken by Ben's abrupt shift in mood. She searched for a sign of his mouth twisting into that familiar teasing curve, but his expression was almost grim. She realized with a start that he was actually hurt that she thought he'd intentionally try to derail her career. This was a side of him that she hadn't seen before. A vulnerable side.

"Where are you going?" she asked, unable to hide the note of concern in her voice.

"Back to work." Now his tone was downright austere.

She couldn't believe he'd walk out on her. Just like that. To her dismay, she also couldn't believe how much she suddenly found herself not wanting him to leave.

"But . . . but you haven't even finished your tea."

He shrugged. "Actually, I hate tea."

He continued heading for the door.

"Ben, wait." Inexplicably, tears threatened to surface. She was stunned by her reaction to his impending departure.

He stopped, turned back and looked directly at her. She saw a muscle in his cheek move, but otherwise his features remained cool and implacable.

"Could you . . . help me get up to my . . . bedroom . . . before you take off? All those . . . stairs. I'm a little nervous . . . trusting to the crutches." *Will you listen to me. I'm seducing him. What's come over me?* she asked herself. *Lust,* a little voice in her head whispered. And then another little voice intruded. *Or could it be "the real thing"*?

While all these thoughts were racing through her mind, Ben was giving her a long, rueful look. "I'd have thought you'd trust those crutches a lot quicker than you'd trust me."

Julie threw up her hands. "Okay, I get the message."

Ben leaned casually against the doorjamb. "What message?"

"This is getting-back-at-Julie time."

Ben's eyes narrowed. "You're really something, Jules."

Well, she thought, at least we're back to "Jules." "And what's that supposed to mean?"

He started to say something, then shook his head. "Never mind."

He turned again to leave.

"Wait," Julie called out. "I think I know what you mean," she added, her voice more subdued.

Ben waited.

Julie exhaled heavily. "I've put all the blame on you for everything that's happened to me since I came back. Well . . . you *are* to blame for some of what happened. You do egg me on, Ben."

He nodded. "I guess that's true."

"Still," she admitted, "I have no business dumping all the blame on you. I've got a big mouth and sometimes I put my foot in it."

Ben's gaze dropped. "It's a lovely foot. The one without the Ace bandage, naturally."

Her heart started to race. "I get carried away sometimes. I . . . lose perspective. I can be . . . very intense."

He smiled now. "That's because you feel things passionately. That's why I've always been drawn to you, Jules."

Spirals of warmth spread through her body. "I have a bad temper."

"Yeah, but you're beautiful when you're angry."

They both smiled at the tired cliché.

"You're just trying to make me feel better," she muttered.

"Sure I am," he agreed softly. He was still smiling, but there was nothing of the tease in the smile. It was one of pure tenderness.

The kitchen seemed to vibrate with new energy. They could both feel it.

Julie tried to fight it. She gave him a wan look. "I don't want to be attracted to you, damn it."

"There are worse things," he murmured.

She sighed. "And I really don't know why you're attracted to me. I'm not exactly a 'gift horse,' Ben."

Ben grinned. "Neither am I."

"Tell me something I don't know," she said dryly.

He folded his arms across his chest, still leaning against the doorjamb. "I love you."

There was silence. Dead silence. Julie didn't know what to say. Her throat went dry. Now the pounding of her heart drowned out the throbbing in her ankle. Why couldn't he have beaten around the bush a little?

Why did he have to come right out with it like that? And did he even mean it?

Her eyes met his. Then she looked away. He meant it. He was in love with her. This was no joke. This was serious. She clamped her hands together. Her palms were sweaty. She shivered despite the August heat. She felt dizzy. The room started to spin.

"Do you still want me to help you up to your bedroom?" Ben asked quietly.

Julie didn't trust her voice. She simply nodded.

As he lifted her into his arms, her own arms curled around his neck. She dropped her head to his shoulder—to his pale blue, much-washed cotton shirt soft and comforting against her cheek. The faint lemony scent of the soap he'd used that morning clung to his skin. He wore no cologne. That pleased her. Jordan always wore very expensive cologne. She hadn't minded at the time, but now she realized how much nicer it was to breathe in the real, earthy scent of a man. And something else came to mind: Jordan had never once carried her off to a bedroom. Then again, she'd never asked him to. She'd never needed to be carried off. Still, it did feel awfully good to be in Ben's strong arms, pressed against his body, feeling the strength and power of his sinewy muscles, breathing him in. There was no artifice about Ben. He was who he was. He was comfortable with himself; in harmony with his own body. That excited her in a way she'd never felt with Jordan. A delicious warmth continued to spread through her.

Neither of them spoke as he carried her out of the kitchen, down the hall, and up the stairs. Only when they got closer to her bedroom door did Julie at last find her voice.

"I never did . . . get that lock," she mumbled, flushing like a schoolgirl.

He smiled, pressing his lips to her hair. "We'll wedge a chair against the door."

THAT MORNING, BEFORE she'd left for her early meeting with Kate—a meeting in which she'd fully intended to once again refuse any further appearances on "Pittsville Patter"—Julie had drawn the curtains in her bedroom. It was now cool and dim there despite the bright hot summer sun beating down on the roof.

Ben laid her gently on the bed, careful of her sprained ankle. He skimmed her cheek with his fingertips after releasing her.

She looked up at him, surprised. "Your hand's trembling."

He smiled gently. "My whole body's trembling, Jules. I'm going to confess something to you. I'm nervous as all get-out."

"So am I," she admitted. She held up her own trembling hands for him to inspect. He took them in his, bringing each in turn, palms up, to his lips.

She smiled tremulously as he planted a kiss on each palm.

"I'd better go wedge that chair against the door."

She nodded.

He didn't move away immediately. His head dipped low and he planted a curiously tentative kiss on her lips. This kiss was different. This kiss was a prelude. In its own way, it caused more of an erotic stirring in Julie than their other, more torrid kisses. When his mouth left hers, her breath escaped in the softest of moans.

"Don't go away," he murmured.

Julie's eyes sparkled. "Is that an order, Sandler?"

His thumb slid seductively across her just-kissed lips. "Yes."

She grinned. "Think you're pretty tough, don't you?"

"Jules," he said beguilingly, "I'm putty in your hands."

"Then take care of that chair, pronto, so I can get my hands on you."

They both laughed a little breathlessly; the light, familiar banter eased their nervousness.

He pulled a ladder-back chair that stood by Julie's desk over to the door and fit the back of it under the knob. There was always a chance Kate or Rachel might come over to check on their injured sister, although Ben was fairly certain that once they spotted his car at the curb they weren't likely to come barging into her room again. Still, better safe than *interrupted!*

When he returned, Julie had begun unbuttoning her white silk blouse.

"Let me," he whispered.

As he undid each button, his fingertips grazed her bare skin. Wherever they touched, her nerve endings instantly responded. Her whole body felt acutely sensitized. Her ankle not only ceased to throb, it practically ceased to exist.

When he finished with the last button, Ben opened her shirt wide, his palms moving in gentle, erotic circles over her bare midriff, and then over the lacy bra covering her breasts. Her taut nipples pressed against the thin material.

She reached up and unbuttoned his shirt, lifting her head from the pillow to press her lips against his lean, muscular chest. Her tongue darted out to taste him. He tasted piercingly good.

They stripped each other this time without calamity and Ben slid down beside her on the narrow bed. They both let out a whoosh of sheer pleasure as their naked bodies met.

Ben began stroking her back, her buttocks, her hips. Her body felt delightfully defined by his ardent caresses.

"I love the feel of you, Jules," he murmured, dipping his hands between her thighs.

"I probably should be working out—"

He stopped her with his lips. "I'll give you a workout you'll never forget."

She laughed. "I don't doubt it," she said lightly, but she meant it. *This will be a memory I'll take with me always.*

She sighed inwardly. *Still one foot out the door,* just as Ben had pointed out to all their viewers. Well, she couldn't help it. Anymore than she could help this. Still, she should tell him. She didn't want him to have any illusions. She didn't want to deceive this man who'd so openly and ingenuously expressed his love for her.

"Ben."

"Mmm?" He was depositing dewy kisses along her hipbone.

"This won't . . . change anything."

"Won't it?" he asked, his hot breath firing up her flesh.

She had to lift his head away from her body for her to be able to get out what she felt she had to say to him. "I mean...I still want what I wanted before I came back here. I still want a second chance at the big leagues."

"Is that it?"

"Yes." A brief pause. "No."

He waited.

"I want...you, Ben."

"Good. Let's start with that."

Gratefully, she nodded. Greedily, she clung to him as he drew her against him, a shuddering sigh fluttering off her lips.

Her hands stroked him, molded him, enfolded him. His tautness pulsated against her fingers. She began licking his skin, gliding her tongue across his nipples, down his chest, circling his belly button, all the while holding him, stroking him.

He groaned loudly—almost a cry. "God, that feels great."

For a fleeting moment it brought to mind how silent a lover Jordan had been. She'd never been quite sure what pleased him. Ben left nothing to doubt.

She felt Ben's hands on her buttocks, tracing patterns on her skin, and all thought of Jordan fled from her. There was only Ben: his hands, his body, his warm breath, his voice, his loving.

He nudged her gently onto her back and slid over her, careful to avoid brushing against her sprained ankle in the process. Julie had all but forgotten the injury. This was better than any painkiller. Sex. The new wonder drug. The miracle cure.

A bittersweet pang hit her. *If only sex was all this was about*... The rest... The rest was a jumble of emotions she couldn't sort out. Didn't want to...

He rose above her, his palms pressed into the mattress so that it dipped beneath his weight. His gaze was riveted on her eyes. In them, Ben saw liquid desire. And something else. Something Julie couldn't give voice to, but something her eyes couldn't conceal. She loved him, too.

She moaned softly as if in confirmation. Still, he knew it would be hell getting her to admit it. To herself, never mind to him.

He hovered over her like a hummingbird. She felt him, moist and throbbing, against her thigh. What was he waiting for?

"It's okay, Ben. I'm on the Pill."

Ben gazed down at her intensely. "Are you sure this is what you want, Jules?"

"If you mean, am I going to blame you later for seducing me, no. No, Ben." Her pulse was racing pell-mell.

His lips moved across her damp brow, her dark-lashed eyes, her hungry, eager, intoxicating mouth.

"Please, Ben. I feel like I'm going to explode," she confessed, her heart hammering against her rib cage. She really did feel she might burst with the sheer wanting.

He smiled down at her. "Not yet, Jules. This is one explosion I want to be part of."

For a few agonizing and yet delicious moments he teased her wantonly, his head dipping so his mouth captured hers, his tongue darting playfully in and out of her mouth.

"Damn you, Ben," she gasped, "can't you take anything seriously...?"

He grinned. "You want serious?"

"Yes. Yes."

He brushed her lips with his, and then, without warning, entered her in one swift slide. "Is this serious, Jules?"

Her breath caught in her throat at the surprise and the exquisiteness of it. "Oh, yes..."

He drew himself up and slipped almost out of her. Julie quickly threw her good leg over him, pinioning him to her so he couldn't stop what he'd started.

"Don't worry, Jules," he assured her tenderly. "I'm not going anywhere."

"Oh," she cried out in ecstasy as he thrust himself inside her again, this time deeper than before.

As she felt him hot, hard, bursting inside her, the warmth that had suffused her earlier turned into a flood of fevered heat. She was burning up. She was on fire.

Meeting each of his thrusts now with equal force and hunger, her cries of pleasure became ragged moans as her whole body began to quake.

Their rhythm intensified, their breathing becoming little more than shallow gulps now.

"Is this the way you want it, Jules?" he murmured hotly against her hair, gripping her buttocks tightly, trying to reach the very depth of her.

"Yes. Oh...yes, Ben." She'd never dreamed he would be such a compelling lover.

His tongue slid across her lips, scorching her. Her fingers grabbed his hair.

"Now, Ben. Now..."

"Yes, Jules..."

They kissed fiercely—a long, drugging kiss—as wave after wave of their mutual climax shuddered through them.

Afterward, they laughed softly as they felt their diaphragms expand and contract heavily against each other's chest.

He nuzzled her neck. "How's your ankle?"

"What ankle?"

He kissed the tip of her nose. An effervescent smile lit her face.

"Was it good for you, Jules?"

"Yes."

He grinned. "I know."

She nudged him playfully. "Then why'd you ask?"

"I just wanted to hear you say it."

"It was better than good," she admitted.

He rolled onto his side, fixing her with his gaze. "How much better?"

She flushed. "A lot better."

His hand slid up her rib cage. "Great?"

"Well..."

He cupped her breast. "Spectacular?"

"You don't ask for much, do you?"

He rolled her nipple between his thumb and his index finger. "Not much."

She emitted a little gasp, amazed that he could arouse her again so soon after making love. "Liar."

His lips captured her now taut nipple. He gave a little tug. "Tell me."

She pressed herself up against him. "Okay... Great."

His hand snaked down between their bodies. His fingers slipped between her thighs. "Go on."

"What? You want more?"

His fingers found their way to her pulsating core. "Yes."

She arched into him. "Will . . . spectacular do?"

"For starters," he said, his tongue licking a circle around each nipple.

"Starters?"

His hands moved down the length of her. "It gets even better."

"Prove it. . . ."

# 6

HANK VARGAS, a short, stocky man in his early thirties with a shock of bright red hair worn pulled back in a ponytail, was one of *Happening*'s star reporters. He had arrived in Pittsville on Saturday afternoon with his cameraman, Jesse Wolfe, a tall, skinny man in blue jeans and a black T-shirt, whose face was hidden for the most part behind his Nikon camera.

Hank sat across from Julie and Ben around the newly arrived oak table and captain's chairs on the "Pittsville Patter" set. Behind them was the new bland hunter-green backdrop. The sign was gone, the name of the show now painted in plain lettering across the top of the backdrop. Julie had been pleased with the renovation. Ben had said very little about it.

Hank looked around, shaking his head. "No, no. This is all wrong."

"What's all wrong?" Julie asked quizzically.

"The set," Hank said. "What'd you do?"

Off to one side of the threesome stood Jesse with his Nikon. He, too, didn't look happy. "Yeah, man. This is like the pits." He grinned crookedly at his partner. "Hey man, get it? The pits? Pittsville?"

"The old set had absolutely no class," Julie said irritably. "We're trying to upgrade the show."

"No, no. It's all wrong," Hank muttered. "We gotta have that sign back, at least. The one that bopped you on the head the first night."

"Yeah, man. Definitely," the cameraman concurred. "I was hoping we could kind of duplicate that shot—"

"Absolutely not," Julie exclaimed, horrified at the very thought.

Hank looked over at Ben, who'd remained uncharacteristically quiet, so far. "Come on, Sandler. You're not going to tell me you actually like this new white-bread look?"

Julie's eyes shot to Ben. He glanced at her, smiled, gave the table a little rap. "Good, solid oak." He slapped the arms of his chair. "Nice, comfortable chairs."

"Yeah, man. The chairs," Jesse muttered. "We need those old chairs back. That was such a gas when that chair Hart was on collapsed."

"And the green backdrop," Ben went on as if he hadn't been interrupted. "Nothing wrong with the color green. We've got green grass, green peas, green...eyes."

"Why don't we forget about the set and get down to the interview," Julie said tightly.

Hank nodded begrudgingly, clearly not happy, and switched on his tape recorder. He looked Ben square in the face. "Come on, Sandler. You and Hart here never agree on anything. So, what's your real take on this new set?"

Julie rolled her eyes.

"Like I said, it's fine," Ben said evenly. He was determined not to let this reporter egg him and Julie into one of their typical battles. After all, he had promised Julie

### *THE READER SERVICE: HERE'S HOW IT WORKS*

Accepting free books puts you under no obligation to buy anything. You may keep the books and gift and return the invoice marked "cancel". If we don't hear from you, about a month later we will send you 4 additional books and invoice you for just £1.99* each. That's the complete price, there is no extra charge for postage and packing. You may cancel at any time, otherwise every month we'll send you 4 more books, which you may either purchase or return - the choice is yours.

*Terms and prices subject to change without notice.

NO
STAMP
NEEDED

Harlequin Mills & Boon
**FREEPOST**
P.O. Box 70
Croydon
Surrey
CR9 9EL

If offer card is missing, write to: Harlequin Mills & Boon,

he'd do everything he could not to mess this interview up for her. If playing it straight was going to give her the chance she wanted to get back in network television, he was going to do his best. Even though he knew he'd be devastated if he lost her.

"Okay, okay, let's leave the set for a minute," Hank said, clearly disappointed.

Julie was just as clearly relieved.

The reporter's eyes fell on her. "So, how'd you sprain your ankle, Hart? You and Sandler get into a little wrestling match off the air?"

Julie turned scarlet. "No," she gasped. "Don't be ridiculous."

"Ridiculous," Ben echoed. "She was doing a cartwheel and—" He stopped short as he caught Julie's glare. "No, wait...I wasn't even there. Not until...later." He cleared his throat. "How did you sprain your ankle, Jul-ie?" *Oops, almost slipped up again.* They'd agreed, before the reporter from *Happening* got there, that he would not use his term of endearment for her in front of him. They were going to behave like pros.

"So, tell me about the cartwheel, Hart," Hank prodded. It was obvious he thought he had tapped into a potentially newsworthy nugget.

"I was simply...exercising," Julie muttered. "I like to keep in shape. Being physically fit helps me think better, be more alert."

"Did I say a cartwheel?" Ben fabricated a confused look. "No, no. I didn't mean 'cartwheel' in that exact sense. I was using it...loosely. Broadly."

Julie wished he would shut up. He was only making it worse.

"I still don't get how you sprained your ankle," Hank said, not about to let her off the hook.

"I got . . . distracted."

Hank raised a bushy red eyebrow in Ben's direction. "Wanna tell me what distracted her, Sandler?"

Ben rubbed his palms together. "I really . . . wouldn't know."

Hank winked. "I think you do. I think you're holding out on me. Give me the real scoop on your new coanchor, Sandler. What makes her tick?"

Ben placed his hands flat on the table. He adjusted the tie that he'd worn for Julie's sake—along with the blue blazer, the chino pants. He felt like a complete phony. And he knew he sounded like one, too. "Julie's an extremely intelligent and committed professional newscaster and interviewer. She's sharp, incisive, and asks the tough questions. She has the ability to . . . shake things up."

Hank grinned. "She's sure shaken you up, hasn't she, Sandler?"

Ben shot Julie a look. She was sitting rigid in her chair, staring straight ahead. Ben looked back at the reporter. "The show's definitely gotten livelier and more . . . involved since Julie became my coanchor."

"Say, man," Jesse interrupted, pointing at Ben. "Could you pull your chair closer to Hart's. I got it. Why don't the two of you mime an arm-wrestling match for me. What do ya think, Hank?"

"Yeah, good," Hank agreed. "We need to get things heated up here."

"I won't do any such thing," Julie snapped. "Look, if you guys merely intend to make us into a pair of battling ninnies, we can stop the interview right here and now."

Hank Vargas reached across and turned off the tape recorder. "I don't think you two get it. I saw those two 'Pittsville Patter' shows on tape. They made one of the hottest hours on TV I've seen in ages. You two are dynamite together. Funny, sexy, pungent. The highbrow dame from D.C. and the down-home country boy. Who'd ever guess the mix would be magic? Now, the thing is, if we're gonna have us a kick-ass interview, you two have gotta loosen up, let things fly. You know what I mean? You get the picture? Otherwise, we're gonna have our readers yawning over this story. It'll sit there on the page like a lead balloon. If it even makes its way into the magazine."

"Right on," Jesse seconded.

Ben looked over at Julie. She sat there, staring off into space, seemingly at a complete loss. Not Ben. He knew what he had to do. For Julie's sake. The question was, would she understand?

"Okay, for starters, this new set stinks," he proclaimed dramatically, slapping his hand down on the table. "It's drab, lifeless, sterile. . . ."

Julie turned to him, stunned. "What? What are you talking about? You . . . you just said . . . not a minute ago . . . that it was fine. You . . . you agreed to . . . to everything."

Hank quickly flicked the tape recorder back on. He winked at his cameraman. Jesse gave a thumbs-up sign.

"Agreed? Jules, I haven't agreed with you since we were in grade school. And the only time I agreed with you back then was when you wanted to stick a wad of gum on Mr. Madison's chair when he wasn't looking. Mr. Madison was our principal," he clarified for Hank.

Julie was speechless, appalled. It felt like she was sitting next to Jekyll and Hyde. What the hell did Ben think he was doing? So much for his promises.

"Why'd you want to put gum on the principal's chair, Hart?" Hank coaxed.

"I . . . I didn't. I never . . ."

Ben raised his eyebrows. "Come on, Jules. You may as well come clean."

"Ben," she spat out between clenched teeth.

Ben merely smiled. "Okay, Hank. This is typical Julie for you. Even back in grade school she was a firebrand. You see, Mr. Madison issued this new dress code that forbade girls from wearing jeans to school. Jules was outraged. She felt Madison was being a typical male chauvinist."

"For heaven's sake," Julie muttered, "this is so juvenile."

"Yeah, yeah." Hank gestured with his hand for Ben to go on.

Ben obliged. "She had this big confrontation with him in his office, but she couldn't budge him. When she stormed out I was sitting out some detention in the outer office—for chewing gum in class. I still had the gum in a wad in my hand."

"So, did you do it?" Hank asked eagerly.

"Naw, Jules chickened out at the last minute."

"I did not chicken out," Julie snapped. "I seem to remember you didn't want to hang around until the coast was clear because it meant missing baseball practice."

"Basketball," Ben corrected genially. "And I only went off to practice because I could see you were losing your nerve."

"I have never lost my nerve."

"You know what my big mistake was?"

Julie's eyes narrowed. She knew what his big mistake was, all right. Existing!

"I should've dared you," Ben said, then turned to Hank. "Dare her and she'll do just about anything. Even a cartwheel."

"Judas," she hissed, sorely tempted to wack Ben with one of her crutches. The only thing that stopped her was seeing the photo of her assault on him splashed across one of the pages of *Happening*.

"This is the crazy thing about me and Jules," Ben said, loosening his tie. "We don't agree on anything, we're complete opposites. And yet we're really crazy about each other."

Julie's face was flooded with fury. "Oh, we're crazy, all right."

Jesse snapped a shot of Julie glaring at Ben.

"See, the thing is," Ben went on blithely, removing the tie altogether, "we often take opposing sides—she leans to the left and I guess you'd say I lean more to the right—but between us we've kind of got the whole area covered. That's what makes us so good together on the show. We give the viewers a chance to see the whole gamut of possibilities. Before Jules came on the scene, the show was pretty hokey at best. Real low-key. Jules goosed things up, really lifted the show to new heights, if you know what I mean. And I guess you know the audience response has been fantastic. Everyone's raving about the show now. Jules here deserves all the credit." He leaned over and planted a kiss on her cheek.

Another flash went off in Julie's face as Jesse snapped the shot.

"I've already got a pretty good idea of what goes on between you two on the air," Hank said with a sly smile. "What our readers would love to know is what goes on between the two of you off the air."

"Nothing," Julie said acidly.

"We're friends," Ben said at the same time.

"Friends?" Hank prompted Ben.

Julie's lips barely moved. "Casual acquaintances."

Ben grinned at Hank. "She's wild about me, but she refuses to admit it."

Julie was wild, all right. She looked like she wanted to strangle him right there on the spot. "That's a complete lie."

To Julie's chagrin, the cameraman caught the look on film.

Meanwhile Ben winked at the reporter. "See what I mean?"

Hank was taking it all in. "So the two of you do battle off the air as well as on the air, huh?"

"You could say that," Ben said, smiling provocatively at Julie.

Hank grinned at her. "You've got a mean right hook, Jules. You swing at him off camera, too?" he goaded her.

"Julie," she corrected, tight-lipped. "Could you please call me Julie. Or Hart. Or anything. Just don't call me Jules. And no, I do not swing at him off camera. I wouldn't waste my time or energy," she added icily.

Ben smiled conspiratorially at the reporter. "I'm pretty much the only one who calls her Jules. You know how it is."

Julie was seething. "I've had just about all I can stand," she snapped, grabbing her crutches from the floor and leaping up from her chair. Unfortunately, in her haste to storm off the set, she miscalculated the clearance between her injured right leg and the thick oak leg of the table. As the two legs collided, she let out an involuntary yelp of pain, lost her balance and went careening backward. Landing right in Ben's lap.

The magazine photographer's flash caught her right in the eye.

"I DID IT FOR YOU, Jules."

"I do not want to speak to you, Ben." She spat out each word as if it were a bullet. "I never want to speak to you again as long as I live. And the way I feel now, it probably won't be very long." Her voice was drained of emotion. She'd had it.

The orthopedist walked into the examing room, the new set of X rays in hand. He gave his patient a sympathetic smile. "Bad news, I'm sorry to say."

Julie smiled sardonically. "There is no other kind, is there?"

"Broken?" Ben asked the doctor anxiously. He really was feeling awful about what had happened.

The orthopedist nodded. "It's only a small fracture, but I'm afraid we'll have to set it and put it in a cast."

"For how long?" Julie asked blandly, the fight knocked out of her. What was one more disaster? Her career was over anyway. By the time the next issue of *Happening* hit the stands, she'd be a national laughingstock. She would never forgive Ben for this. Never!

"We'll check it in four weeks," the doctor was saying solicitously. "If you're lucky—"

"Lucky? Right. I'll probably break my other leg before that," Julie said dryly. She shot Ben a lethal look. "And somebody else's head."

"DID YOU SEE THE LATEST?" Kate said, excitement and expectation in her voice, as she swung into a booth at the Full Moon Café beside Rachel and across from Julie, who was sitting sideways so that she could prop her broken leg across the bench seat.

Kate plunked the television-trade newsletter down on the gray-and-green Formica table, tapping an article in the bottom right-hand column.

Julie, still despondent over the farce of an interview she'd had with the reporter from *Happening*—not to mention her broken leg—and still furious at Ben whom she blamed for both catastrophes, glanced at the article halfheartedly. A familiar name sprang out at her: Jordan Hammond.

Instantly interested, she snatched up the paper and read the article. "What? ABC isn't picking up the option on 'News and Views'?" She was totally perplexed. "I don't get it. It was one of the top-rated news interview shows last year. Jordan was sure he'd have a five- or six-year run with it."

"That was when you were his coanchor," Kate said with a smile.

Rachel nodded as she munched on a large order of fries. "Obviously his new coanchor was a dud."

Julie frowned as she kept reading. "Unfortunately, Jordan comes up smelling like roses once again. It says here there's a new show in the works for him." She looked up again. "Figures. He always lands on his feet." She stared at her cast. "I'll bet he never broke a single bone in his whole perfect body."

"You aren't still carrying a torch for Jordan Hammond, are you?" Kate asked incredulously.

"Not for Jordan. Not for any man," Julie said emphatically. "I'm through with the whole lot of them. If I was blind and crippled, I wouldn't trust a one of them to get me safely across the street. Especially if his name was Ben Sandler."

"I think you're being too hard on Ben. He feels awful about your leg," Rachel said.

"My leg, nothing. He made a complete mockery of that magazine interview. He made me look like an absolute idiot. And after he swore he'd behave. After we—" Julie's mouth clamped shut, tiny red splotches springing out on her cheeks.

Her two sisters honed in on her. "After you...what?" Kate prodded.

Rachel grinned, her eyes sparkling. "Bet I can guess."

"Oh, really, this whole dumb town seems to be populated by nothing but juveniles," Julie said haughtily.

"Speaking of juveniles," Kate said as her daughter came racing breathlessly into the café waving a magazine.

"Wait till you see!" Skye cried out excitedly. "You won't believe it!"

"I'd believe anything at this point," Julie said dryly.

Skye grinned. "Oh yeah? Do you believe this?" She held the magazine up high with two hands so the cover faced Julie. Kate and Rachel both leaned forward to get a look, too.

The mouths of all three sisters gaped open.

There on the cover of the latest issue of *Happening* was a photo of Julie on Ben's lap right after she'd slammed her bum leg into the table leg. What had been agony on her face from the pain, looked more like ecstasy in the photo. As for Ben's face, it radiated a mix of surprise, concern, and pleasure. The headline across the bottom of the cover read: Hart and Sandler Make the Local Airwaves Sizzle. . . .

THE NEXT DAY WAS sheer chaos at WPIT. Phones were ringing off the hook; the sacks of mail were piled out in the hall. On their way over to the studio, Julie and Ben had both been accosted by hordes of locals and summer visitors, all scrambling for autographs, snapping photographs, bombarding them with questions. Someone even swiped Ben's Red Sox cap as a souvenir. Julie clung to her crutches, terrified someone would accidentally knock her over and she really would end up breaking her other leg.

The warring pair met up in the hallway of WPIT. They stared at each other in silence. Ben finally broke it.

"How's your leg?" he asked solicitously.

Julie struggled to remain cool and poised—not an easy feat either physically or mentally. "Okay."

Ben cleared his throat. "I guess you saw the new issue of *Happening*."

Julie nodded slowly.

"Jules . . ."

She held up her hand, and without another word, turned on her crutches and swung her way into Kate's office.

Ben stood there, watching her disappear.

"She'll cool down," Rachel said, coming up behind him.

"The interview was going nowhere," Ben said forlornly. "I took a chance. I did it for her."

"I thought it was a great story. And, hey, you landed the cover," Rachel said, patting him on the back.

"I promised her I wouldn't screw things up for her."

"You haven't," Rachel said with a bright smile. "Just the opposite, in fact."

He gave her a closer look. "What do you mean?"

"Kate's been fielding job offers for Julie all morning. Suddenly, the pariah of the networks has become a hot property."

Ben didn't know what to say. This was what Julie wanted. And he'd contributed to it happening. He should feel good for her. He did. It was himself he felt sorry for.

"The networks are interested in you, too. This could be your big opportunity, Ben."

He stared at her, nonplussed. "An opportunity for what? There's no place I want to go, Rachel. This is my home. I've never made any bones about wanting national celebrity or a pressure-cooker job in some big city. Things are pretty much the way I want them to be." There was only one thing missing—or she would be missing at some point soon, now.

Rachel smiled sympathetically. "You really do love her, don't you?"

Ben sighed. "I guess that's pretty obvious."

"I do have one piece of potentially good news."

"What's that?" he asked listlessly.

"Kate's also got several offers to put 'Pittsville Patter' into syndication."

Ben was taken aback. "You're kidding?"

"No. It's the truth. Naturally, if stations agreed to buy the show they'd want a commitment that the co-anchors would be around for a while. Meaning from you and Julie. Kate figures you'd both have to sign on for at least two years."

The corners of Ben's mouth turned down. "Oh, sure. The networks are ready to roll out the red carpet for Julie and she's going to turn them all down for a co-anchor spot with me on 'Patter' for two years in syndication?"

"Don't write her off yet, Ben. Love's a pretty powerful motivator. I know."

"You know? You mean Jules has said something to you?"

"No. No, not in so many words," Rachel admitted, seeing the disappointment flash across Ben's face. "I meant I know what it's like to be in love. And I'm willing to put my money on Julie being in love with you, whether she's ready to admit it yet or not."

Ben sighed wistfully. "Even if that's true, love's not the only motivator. Not for someone like Jules. There's also ambition. And sweet revenge. If Julie takes a network show she ends up with the last laugh."

Rachel remained optimistic. "To paraphrase my favorite male anchor, you can't curl up in bed beside a career or a 'last laugh.'"

"WE'D LIKE THE opportunity to wine you and dine you, Miss Hart. Granted, Toledo isn't Washington, D.C., but 'Toledo Talks' is a top-ranked show and we don't have the pressures here, the crime, the awful summer heat. . . ."

"I've never minded the heat, Miss Raskin."

"That's Ruskin. Anne Ruskin. We could fly you out here first class at your earliest convenience, Miss Hart."

"Why don't I get back to you, Miss Raskin. . . ."

Julie hung up the phone, a big smile on her face.

"You're loving this, aren't you?" Kate said. She was perched on a corner of her desk, which was strewn with memos, mail and paperwork.

"A couple of weeks ago, that snotty little producer was giving me the bum's rush," Julie said. "Let her see how it feels."

Kate handed her sister a stack of memos. "What about all these?" Kate didn't mention the dozens of requests from major markets all over the country requesting that she offer "Pittsville Patter" for syndication. Putting a show into syndication was an expensive deal, but she'd received interest from several financial sources that would consider backing her efforts to make and distribute the show for national sales.

In her wildest dreams, Kate couldn't imagine Julie opting for a "Patter" with Ben instead of signing on for a high-paying, high-status network show. And she didn't want Julie to feel she should do it for her. For WPIT. Kate, in no way, wanted Julie to feel beholden to her. And the truth was, Julie had already done more than her part in helping put WPIT in the black for the first time since Kate had taken over the station. Sponsors, both local and national, were snatching up all the advertising time the station had to sell. Even if Julie left at this point, Kate felt confident that WPIT would remain solvent.

Julie took the slew of memos in hand and started sorting through them. She pursed her lips. Producers from a number of network news and entertainment interview shows were eager to have a chat with her. "Gee, it's nice to be sought-after for a change. I never dreamed . . . I never expected . . . I was sure that interview in *Happening* would finish me off. And now . . ." Guiltily, she stared at the memos, then slapped them down on the desk.

"Where are you going?" Kate asked as she watched her sister lurch across the office on her crutches.

"To eat humble pie," Julie mumbled.

Kate grinned. "Well, if it's any consolation, it'll probably taste better than the mincemeat-custard pie Meg Cromwell's concocted for this week's show."

JULIE FOUND BEN in his garret office on the third floor. She was a little breathless from having dragged herself up the two flights on her crutches.

She stood nervously at the open door trying to steady her breathing. Ben was at his desk, reading. Either he didn't notice her, or he chose to pretend not to. She cleared her throat. "Boy, this place is a madhouse today."

Ben slowly looked up from a sheaf of notes. "Yeah, it is pretty crazy," he said, eyeing her guardedly.

She hesitated, shifting her weight. The "humble pie" wasn't going to be so easy to get down. "This is all your doing, you know."

Ben rose from his chair, walked around his desk toward her. "You want to punch me out?"

She smiled sheepishly. "No. No, I don't want to punch you out. I'm really not a violent person, Ben Sandler, and you know it."

He came a little closer. "So, what do you want?"

She smiled tentatively. "What I want is . . ." A lot of "wants" flooded into her head, but none of them were the ones she dared express. "I want to thank you."

"You do?" He didn't sound altogether convinced.

Julie shifted her weight again. She wished Ben would stop staring at her like he was. She wished he wasn't standing so close to her. It was hard to concentrate on what she wanted to say. "That article in *Happening* would have been dull as dishwater if we'd played it my way. Or, as Vargas said, it might not even have been worth printing. All the interest in me that's being stirred up again . . . Well, I owe it all to you, Ben."

Was that a flicker of a smile she saw on his face. She took heart.

"It's what you wanted," he said softly.

She nodded slowly. "Yes." She hesitated. "Not that I'm rushing into anything yet. The ball's in my court now."

"Right. Play hard-to-get. Good strategy."

Their eyes met and held.

Julie felt her throat go dry. "What kind of strategy do I use with you, Ben?"

He compressed his lips. "Just say what's on your mind."

She laughed softly. "That would take a long time."

"I'm in no hurry."

She looked around the office, then returned her gaze to his face. "Not here."

"Where?"

She hesitated. "What about my dad's hunting lodge up in Harmon? We could . . . pack a few things, pick up some groceries and spend . . . a couple of days . . . just relaxing, talking... We don't really have to be back until Wednesday, for the show. . . ."

Julie waited expectantly for some kind of response from Ben. The silence stretched. Her discomfort mounted.

She tried for a nonchalant shrug—not an easy feat, considering the crutches. "It was . . . just a suggestion," she muttered. "Only because... Well, I thought it would be a good idea... to get out of town for a few days... until things settle down a little. Everywhere we go around here . . . we'll be swamped with autograph hounds. So I just thought . . ."

Ben was so close she could feel his breath on her face. Still, he said nothing. Frustration got the better of her.

"Okay, I deserve this," she declared.

"What do you deserve?"

"The cold shoulder."

She started to turn away. Given all the times she'd felt like a fool since her arrival back in Pittsville, she'd never felt more foolish than she did at that moment.

Ben caught hold of one of her crutches, halting her progress. "Where are you going?"

She stared at him forlornly. "In circles," she admitted.

A moment's hesitation and then that knockout smile lit his face. "Me, too."

He cupped her face in his hands. Julie didn't say a word. She hardly took a breath. She simply stared at him expectantly.

"Let's blow this joint," he whispered against the side of her face.

Julie expelled a sigh of sheer relief.

LEO HART'S HUNTING lodge was really a one-room cabin perched on a knoll high up on a winding mountain road in the town of Harmon, which was a couple of hours north of Pittsville. Leo hardly ever used it anymore since his girlfriend, Mellie, had a strong aversion to the sport of hunting. Still, on the few occasions they had gone up there for a weekend getaway, Mellie had felt compelled to spruce up the place. Red-and-white gingham curtains covered the windows. There was a homey oval rag rug in front of the woodstove that sat in the center of the room. Colorful throws adorned the worn old couch and two armchairs that made up the small sitting area. The double bed at the far side of the cabin looked cosy and cheerful covered with the patchwork quilt Mellie had stitched herself.

Ben insisted Julie make herself comfortable on the couch while he carried in the bags of groceries from the car and set about putting them away in the small kitchenette.

Even though it was August, there was a chill in the air and Julie tugged the cotton throw around her shoulders.

"I'll make a fire," Ben suggested, eyeing the neatly stacked logs beside the woodstove. "Then I'll put up something for us to eat."

"No, you deal with lunch and I'll tend to the stove. It's kind of fussy," Julie said.

"You sure?"

"I've lit this stove a hundred times."

"With a busted leg?"

"I don't usually light the match with my feet."

He grinned. "Okay, okay." He spied a fishing rod near the front door. A short distance behind the house was a brook. "Say, maybe I'll catch us a trout for lunch."

"Sounds good," Julie said brightly. "As long as you clean and cook it."

"No problem," Ben said enthusiastically.

He paused at the door, glancing back at Julie, who'd hobbled her way over to the stove and was sorting through logs. "You sure you don't need any help?"

"I know it's hard to believe, but I really am a very competent person, Ben."

He grinned, still making no move to leave.

Julie looked over at him, puzzled as to why he was still standing there. "What's wrong?" she asked.

"Nothing. Nothing's wrong," he said softly. "This was a good idea. Getting away. Spending some time alone together. It's a . . . first for us."

Julie could hear the wistfulness in his tone. Was he thinking this might be the *last* for them, as well? Was he right? Admittedly, she hadn't thought past these few days together.

Julie was suddenly besieged by a bout of second thoughts. Maybe this romantic little getaway wasn't such a good idea, after all. She hadn't thought of the ramifications. She hadn't thought about afterward. She hadn't thought, period. She'd simply wanted to be with him. She wanted to make love with him again. She wanted to feel his warmth, his tenderness. She needed someone and she wanted that someone to be Ben.

"You'd better get fishing or we'll be eating that trout for tomorrow's breakfast," she said, suddenly finding it hard to keep back a rush of threatening tears.

He tapped his fingers against the fishing rod. He could see the struggle on her face. He had a pretty good idea what was going through her mind—the same things that were going through his mind.

She waved him off.

He nodded. "Right. Don't want to keep those trout waiting."

"See you soon," she called as he headed out the door.

He threw her a kiss.

She reached her hand up as if to catch it as he scooted outside.

After the door closed, Julie brought her hand to her lips. A little shiver traveled through her. Her gaze fell on the woodstove. Time to get a fire going.

BEN WAS HAVING his problems catching a trout. He'd rolled up his pants and was standing in the middle of the brook when he heard a faint cry behind him. He spun around and saw smoke billowing not only from the chimney of the cabin but from the windows, as well.

In his panic to get to Julie, he lost his footing on a slippery rock and fell headfirst into the water. Sputtering and coughing, he abandoned the fishing pole and went racing out of the brook and burst into the cabin only to run smack into a cloud of pungent smoke.

"It's okay. Don't panic. Everything's under control," Julie tried to assure him as she threw open the last of the windows.

"What happened?" he asked anxiously, running over to her.

"I guess I forgot to open the damper," Julie said sheepishly. "It's okay, though. It's open now. It'll just take a few minutes for the smoke to clear out."

Ben scooped her up in his arms and carried her outdoors. She was covered from head to cast in black soot. Ben bit back a smile.

"Go on," Julie said. "Laugh. I know I look ridiculous." It was only then that she really looked at him. "You look pretty ridiculous yourself. What were you doing? Diving for trout?"

Now it was Ben's turn to look sheepish. "I fell in the brook."

Julie pressed her lips together.

"Go on," he said. "Laugh. You know you want to."

They both began laughing at the same time. They slid down on the cool green grass outside the smoky cabin, still laughing. The laughter didn't stop until their lips met. Before the smoke had time to fully clear from the cabin, Ben's wet clothes lay mixed in a heap with Julie's sooty things out there on the grass.

Not far from the pile of discarded clothing, Julie lay wrapped in Ben's arms, their naked bodies pressing together. Earlier she'd been shivering. Now, the chill in the mountain air faded as his fiery embrace heated her through and through.

Impatience and need drove them both.

She looked into his eyes. "Oh, Ben . . ." She wanted to say more, but she couldn't. Her feelings were still a jumble. Except for this incredible desire for him.

Ben ran his fingers through her hair. "Yeah, Jules," he whispered.

Her lips rushed to meet his lips. They kissed passionately. She felt him grow and throb against her.

"I can't . . . wait," she whispered hungrily.

Neither could Ben. His heart was hammering. His pulse was roaring. He was desperate to possess her.

She stroked his back, his buttocks, urging him on. She held her breath. Her body was trembling all over.

They cried out in mutual pleasure and abandon as he entered her without further preamble. He needed to be inside her. He needed to fill her. He needed to feel enveloped by her.

"Jules. Jules . . ."

Julie relished the feel of him inside her body. Inside her mind.

His mouth covered hers with a rough and hungry kiss. Her fingers dug into his shoulders. This was what she wanted; what she needed. If only it could be all she wanted and needed. If only it could be enough . . .

She shut her eyes tightly, determined to give herself up completely to the moment. She didn't want to think about all those doors starting to open up for her. Not now. She wanted to shut every single one of them for the time being, and just stay hidden away here in the wilderness with Ben. No distractions. No pressures. No decisions to be made. That was for later. Later, when she could think straight, be logical, sensible, practical.

"Ben. Oh, Ben . . ."

She clung to him, matching thrust for thrust, feeling wild and free, as he carried her with him over the precipice into blissful oblivion. Even after the last wave rippled through her body, she held on tight, her face burrowed against his shoulder.

Ben's grip on her was equally fierce. Maybe if he held on tight enough, long enough, she'd realize that this was where she belonged.

Long minutes passed before he spoke. "Would two years really be pure hell for you, Jules?"

She drew her head back and looked up at him with a blank expression. "Two years?"

Then it dawned on him. "Kate didn't tell you."

Julie remained in the dark. "Tell me what?"

Ben hesitated. It didn't take a genius to figure out why Kate hadn't said anything to Julie.

"Please, Ben. What's this about?" Julie pressed.

Ben realized there was no keeping it from her. "A number of major markets are interested in having Kate put 'Pittsville Patter' into syndication. With the two of us as coanchors, naturally."

"She doesn't have the kind of money—"

"No, but she could get it. Several financial groups are interested in backing her."

"That's . . . incredible. A tiny independent station producing a show for syndication. That's unprecedented."

Ben looked away. "We'd have to agree to a two-year stint. Otherwise, it wouldn't be worth the investment."

Julie was still trying to digest the idea of "Patter" going into syndication. How many local shows ever made it into a national market? None that Julie could think of at the moment.

She shook her head. "Kate didn't say a word to me. Not one word."

Ben shrugged. "I guess she figured, what with all the major-league offers you were getting—"

"She should have told me."

Ben gave her a close look. "Does that mean . . . ?"

"I don't know what it means," she said hurriedly. "I guess it could mean a lot for WPIT. For Kate." She looked into Ben's eyes. "For you."

"You know Kate would never tolerate you doing something like that for her or the station. She'd want you to do what you wanted to do." He stroked her cheek. "Ditto for me, Jules."

Julie nodded. She knew it was true. Neither Ben nor Kate would want her to feel pressured or obligated. They'd support her doing whatever it was she wanted to do. Now all she had to do was figure out what it was she wanted.

# 7

"HOW'S YOUR SALMON? If you don't like it . . . or you prefer something else . . . ?"

"The salmon's fine," Julie assured Daryl Milton, the executive producer of "Feature Players," a top network entertainment-news show.

Julie and Milton were lunching at La Beau Monde, a trendy new four-star Manhattan restaurant, already famous after less than two months for its salmon *en croûte*. Daryl had insisted Julie had to try it, so he'd ordered the dish for both of them. Julie didn't care. Food was the last thing on her mind.

"I'm not sure I understand this new slant you want to give to your show," she said after dutifully sampling a bite of her extravagant and expensive dish.

Milton, sleek and suave in his mid-fifties, smoothed back his impeccably cut graying hair. "Well, it's hard to put into a few words." He paused as if searching for some of them. "I think 'Players' could benefit from more . . . spontaneity, more of a sense of humor." His cheeks reddened. "More . . . sex."

Julie gave him a wary look. "More sex?"

"Julie, Julie. You know what I mean. The kind of thing you and Sandler do so well."

Julie nearly choked on an asparagus tip and started to cough. Milton quickly handed her her water glass.

Julie took several swallows, finally getting her cough under control.

"Are you okay?" he asked anxiously.

She dabbed at her mouth with her napkin and nodded faintly.

Milton relaxed. He returned to his salmon, took a bite, waving his fork in her direction as he chewed and swallowed. "Now Carol Williams is a fine anchorwoman, but, off the record, we don't think she and Joe Prince really. . . click on camera. She lacks your spark. Hell, your fire. And that sock-it-to-you punch. Literally and figuratively. Anyway, Carol's contract comes up for renewal the first of the year and, well . . . I think you and Prince could make magic together, Julie. We'd like to get a commitment from you—"

"Whoa. I'm not ready to make a commitment to anyone," Julie said, thinking to herself that truer words were never spoken. Professionally or personally.

"Julie, Julie. You think I don't understand that? Of course, I understand. Naturally, you'll need a little time. The point I want to make is that we are willing to be very. . . generous," he said, giving her a pointed look. "*Very* generous. And surely I don't have to tell you that 'Feature Players' is one of the top-rated shows of its kind right across the board. I'm talking network and cable."

"I'm basically just looking at all of my options right now, Daryl." *Daryl.* He'd insisted, right from the start, that she call him by his first name. Julie had to smile to herself. Even in her brief heyday at "News and Views" she had never been on a first-name basis with Bill Nesbitt, her executive producer there. This was a whole new ball game. Never had she dreamed she'd be wooed quite like this by the big brass. So why wasn't she enjoying it more?

The producer leaned closer to her. "Is it Prince? I'll be frank with you, Julie. We know he's a little . . . stiff. That he lacks Sandler's irascible charm, but he does have a fine track record and our sponsors love him and he's got an ironclad contract that won't be up for another three years."

"Joe Prince is a fine anchor," Julie said. "I have nothing against him." She set her fork down. "I think you should know, Daryl, that I'm not particularly interested in trying to duplicate the 'magic,' as you call it, on the next show I tackle. I'm a serious news anchor and I want to do serious news and analysis—whether it's in politics, hard news, entertainment, whatever. What's happened on 'Pittsville Patter' has been purely... unintentional."

"Julie, Julie. Any of a dozen of the top anchorwomen around can be 'serious,' as you put it. If we wanted 'serious' we could keep Carol on. We want more sparks, more spice, more—"

"Farce?" Julie suggested glibly. "Maybe you'd like me to break my other leg for the viewers? Or Joe Prince could throw a pie in my face at the end of the show. Hey, that could be our signature sign-off. We could go with a different pie filling each time. . . ."

"Julie, Julie. You've got me all wrong. We're not talking slapstick here. . . ."

"Right. I forgot. We're talking sex."

"Julie, Julie . . ."

"A DIFFERENT COSTUME each week," Susan Bettinger, a wafer-thin mid-twenties network executive with a perfectly coiffed blond shag and an Armani suit was saying to Julie over lunch at The Unicorn, a chic L.A. dining spot two days later.

Julie looked up from her barely touched veal with wild mushrooms and stared at her. "Costume? I don't think I follow."

"Oh, that's the wonderful twist of 'Witness to Yesterday.' You and Sam Becker will don costumes of the period while you're interviewing famous political figures of the past. There'll be Julius Caesar, Queen Victoria, General Custer, both Bobby and John F. Kennedy—"

"Won't that be difficult?" Julie interjected.

Susan was perplexed. "Difficult?"

"I don't know how to break this to you, Sue, but they're all . . . dead."

Susan trilled a fake little laugh. "How droll, Julie. But seriously. . ."

"SERIOUSLY. ANIMALS?" Julie's foot started tapping under the table at Chanticleer, an elegant little D.C. bistro a stone's throw from the Capitol.

"Naturally, you'll be interviewing their owners—not the pets themselves. Unless we dig up a politician who's got a parrot. Only kidding. Only kidding."

Julie managed a wilted smile.

"Not to worry. It's only one small segment of the show, Julie," Nat Wagner, a top network executive assured her over their chilled bowls of vichyssoise. "Politicians' pets will go seven minutes, tops. Our lineup already is mighty impressive, if I do say so myself. We've already got Senator Moore of Illinois and his sheepdog, Shep, slated for our first show. Then there's Representative April Mills and her Persian cat, Truffles. Oh, and we're working on Ambassador Pete Atkinson and his twin gerbils. . . .

"Gerbils?"

"Tom and Jerry. Cute, huh?"

This time Julie didn't even bother trying to manufacture a smile.

Wagner, a big bear of a man, grinned, wagging a finger at her. "I know what you're thinking. Gerbils don't have much personality, but that's where you come in, Julie."

*This,* Julie thought, *is where I go out!*

RACHEL WAS SNACKING on some leftover macaroni and cheese in Kate's kitchen when Julie showed up at her sister's house.

"When did you get back?" Kate asked. She was standing at the sink, finishing up the dinner dishes while Skye was wiping down the table.

"About an hour ago," Julie said wearily.

Rachel pulled out a seat next to her. "How'd it go?"

Julie hobbled over to it on her crutches. "Don't ask."

Skye opened her mouth, but before she could utter a word, she felt her mother staring her down. Skye sighed. "I know. I know. Grown-up time."

Julie ruffled her niece's hair. "I'll fill you in later, kiddo."

"The whole scoop?"

"Soup to nuts." She grinned. "Or chilled vichyssoise to salmon *en croûte,* as it were."

Skye made a face. Cold soup and fish. Not her idea of being wined and dined, that was for sure.

"Since you're being booted out, you may as well clean up your room," Kate called out as Skye reluctantly shuffled out of the kitchen.

"I will. Later," Skye called back.

Kate lifted her eyes to the ceiling. "Later. The cry of the teenager."

"So?" Rachel said, focusing on Kate. "What is the scoop?"

Julie recounted the highlights—or as she coined them, the "lowlights"—of her four days of top-television-exec meetings. Kate and Rachel found themselves laughing practically nonstop. The gerbils really got them. Tears were rolling down Rachel's cheeks and she was holding her extended stomach.

"Stop or I'm going to deliver this baby right here in this kitchen," she said between shrieks of laughter.

"Well, I don't think gerbils are very funny," Julie said petulantly.

"Right. That's where you come in," Kate said, bursting out with another snort of laughter in which she was quickly joined by Rachel.

Julie sat there, stone-faced. She was not the least bit amused and she didn't appreciate the laughs her sisters were having at her expense.

"Oh, come on, Julie. Politicians' pets. It is funny," Kate cajoled.

"No, wait, the costumes are funnier," Rachel said, giggling. "Can you just picture Julie in a toga, reclining on a chaise, munching grapes while she interviews Julius Caesar?"

Kate began laughing harder than before. "How about Julie decked out à la Pocahontas while she interviews Myles Standish?"

Julie cracked a wisp of a smile. "I once dressed up as an Indian princess for Halloween and I didn't look half bad."

Kate came up behind her and squeezed her shoulders. "You're right. I remember. That was the year I dressed up as a pirate and Rachel insisted on going as a penguin."

"Say, I wonder if any politician has a pet penguin," Rachel said with a wiseacre grin.

"Wait," Kate said, raising her hand. "What about Admiral Peary, the first explorer to reach the North Pole?"

"You're getting your shows mixed up," Julie said dryly. "'Witness to Yesterday' doesn't have a dead pets segment."

"Yet," Rachel retorted with a new bout of the giggles.

"I've got it. The ultimate segment," Kate said, laughing again. "Famous dead people's famous dead-pet tricks."

"Great, great," Rachel said, laughing harder.

Julie narrowed her eyes. "Are you two finished?"

Kate and Rachel looked sheepish.

"Sorry," Rachel mumbled, biting her lower lip to keep from laughing again.

"Yes, sorry," Kate said, trying her best to sound contrite as her hand clamped over her mouth to stop another laugh from escaping. "Sorry, sorry. It was just the image of you in that toga. . . ."

Julie waved her hand in the air. "If you want a really big laugh, I've saved the best for last."

Both sisters instantly sobered up, their eyes glued expectantly on Julie.

"I'm considering," Julie announced airily, "taking the 'Patter' syndication deal."

Kate and Rachel shared an incredulous look. Then they resumed staring at Julie, no hint of as much as a smile on either of their faces.

Kate sat down at the table, across from Julie. "It's a joke, right?"

"No, but I grant you it's worth a good laugh."

"Why, I think that's great," Rachel said as the shock began to wear off. "You and Ben . . . together . . . doing the show . . . and everything."

"I'm not ready to sign on the dotted line yet," Julie added hurriedly. "But if I don't get a really good offer within the next few weeks, I'll be ready to talk turkey."

Kate's eyes sparkled. "Turkey?"

Rachel grinned. "Turkey?"

The corners of Julie's mouth twitched. "Did I say turkey?"

Kate's eyes sparkled. "Didn't I read somewhere that Benjamin Franklin had a pet turkey?"

The next instant all three sisters were laughing hysterically.

Skye stuck her head in the door. "What's so funny?"

They were all laughing too hard to answer.

"Really," Skye said with teenage indignation. "If the three of you could hear yourselves. You sound like a gaggle of geese."

"Geese," Kate sputtered, and the threesome began laughing even harder.

*August 14*

I'm beginning to wonder if Aunt Julie isn't having some kind of mental breakdown. When she told me that she actually might stick with "Pittsville Patter" and then gave me this big spiel about how going into syndication might really be a smart move for her, not to mention for Mom, the station, and Ben, I couldn't believe it. Okay, so interviewing politicians' pets or actors playing famous dead people aren't the most scintillating—Aunt Julie's word—assignments for an anchor, but "Feature Players" is definitely up there. I watch the show all the time, and I'm with that producer who made Julie eat fish. Carol Williams is a dud. Whenever she looks at Joe Prince, her mouth puckers. Like she's chewing sour grapes.

I think I know the real reason Aunt Julie isn't interested in taking over her spot, though. I think it's because deep down Joe Prince reminds her of Jordan Hammond. Joe Prince certainly reminds me a lot of Jordan Hammond. They've got that same super-dude manner, like they think they're so-o-o cool they're hot. They even look a little bit alike and dress alike.

Aunt Rachel's convinced Aunt Julie's sticking around because she's fallen head over heels in love with Ben.

My friend Alice says she's just on the rebound and poor Ben's going to end up getting his heart broken.

Alice still has a mad crush on Ben, but she won't admit it. She says she's "past that sort of childish thing." If she's "past" it, why does she still keep that signed photo of Ben pinned up on her wall over her bed? Oh, she'd remembered to take it down before I slept over the other night, but the next day while she was out I stopped back there to pick up a jacket I'd forgotten, and there it was, Ben's picture, right there on her wall. Not that I said anything to her about it. I told my mom, though, and she said she thought that was very mature of me not to rub it in. Then she gave me one of those special "mother-daughter moment" smiles and said in this real wistful way how I really was growing up.

Mom's worried. Not about me. About Aunt Julie. She's worried that Aunt Julie is staying here and doing the show partly for her. I didn't tell her that Aunt Julie said as much to me. The thing is, having "Pittsville Patter" go into syndication really would bring in a lot of money—or revenue, as Mom calls it—for the station. Not that we'd be really rich or anything, but Mom would be able to pay the bills each month without those frown lines popping up across her forehead.

And then there's Ben. No secret that he's madly in love with Aunt Julie. And ever since that story about them came out in *Happening,* Aunt Julie sure has changed her tune about Ben. Now it's, "Ben is so sensitive, so bright, so intuitive." Now, all of a sudden, he's got "irrepressible charm." I don't know, though. She used to say all kinds of flattering things about Jordan

Hammond once upon a time. She even talked about marrying him. She hasn't said a word about wanting to marry Ben. Not that he's asked her yet, but I'm sure he's just trying to get up the courage. I'll bet anything he proposes to her right on TV.

What if Alice is right and Aunt Julie's just taken up with Ben on the rebound? What if he asks her to marry him and she turns him down? He'll be devastated. If Jordan Hammond were to call Aunt Julie tomorrow and say he wanted her back, would she dump poor Ben on the spot and go running back to her "true love"?

*August 15*

This is INCREDIBLE! I swear I must be psychic. Alice wouldn't believe I could "grasp the future" until I finally relented and showed her the last line of yesterday's journal entry. She literally gasped. "You really must have known he would call," she said to me in awe. Because, incredible as it seems, Jordan Hammond truly did call my Aunt Julie this very morning.

And there's more. He's coming to Pittsville. Tomorrow.

When I told Alice, she kept saying, "Poor Ben. Poor Ben." Then she asked me what I thought was going to happen. I guess now that she really does think I could be psychic, she wasn't just asking my "opinion."

I told her I didn't know for sure, but I do have this "funny feeling"—psychic vibes?—that nothing good is going to come of this new turn of events. Mom and

Aunt Rachel agree with me—I overheard them talking on the phone. Maybe they're psychic, too.

As for Aunt Julie, no word as to her reaction yet. But I'll keep my ear to the ground. . . .

# 8

JULIE DECIDED TO TAKE Ben out for lunch and tell him about Jordan's phone call. The last person in the world she expected to find in his office was Jordan Hammond. Her sharp gasp of surprise as she stood at Ben's open door made both men turn to stare at her at the same instant.

Julie's eyes shot furtively from her present lover to her former lover. A study in contrasts if ever she saw one. There was Ben, scruffy leather sandals on his bare feet, untucked button-down shirt hanging over his blue jeans, his blond hair tousled from the habit he sometimes had of combing his fingers through it. And there was Jordan, the anchorman's anchor in his impeccably tailored blue serge suit, the designer tie, the custom dress shirt, Bali tasseled loafers shined to perfection. Socks, naturally. They looked like the silk ones she'd gotten him last Christmas. And was that a little more gray dye at the temples?

"Julie. Darling. Crutches? A cast? Good God!" Jordan exclaimed dramatically.

Julie had to smile. She'd almost forgotten that shorthand style of speech of his—a miser with words when he wasn't being paid to utter them.

He hurried over to her. She turned her head away to dodge the kiss she saw heading for her lips. It landed just above her right ear.

He riveted his gaze on her. "How?"

"I collided with a table leg."

"Come sit down," he insisted, taking hold of her arm.

She waved Jordan off. "I do better... on my own. Thanks."

She didn't, however, make a move. "What are you doing here, Jordan?"

He looked perplexed. "I told you I was coming, Julie."

"No, I mean *here?* In... this office?" Her eyes shot nervously to Ben, whose face bore no sign of what he was thinking. She hoped he wasn't thinking that there were still any lingering feelings between her and Jordan. There certainly weren't. At least on her part.

"I wanted to meet your dynamic coanchor," Jordan said easily. "Naturally, I read the piece in *Happening.* And immediately got my hand on a tape of your shows together." He smiled at Julie. "Damn impressive stuff."

"Right," Julie said dryly. "Just your cup of tea."

"No, really," Jordan insisted, glancing back at Ben. "Bold, dynamic, unconventional. It's the new wave, folks."

Julie gave Ben a sly smile, but he didn't smile back.

"I tell you what," Jordan said, checking his watch. "Lunch on me. Both of you. You pick the spot. Chinese, Japanese, Thai. I'm game for anything."

"Well... Ben and I... That is, I came up here to—"

Ben cut in before she finished. "It'll have to be just you and Julie. I brought a sandwich in with me," he said in a flat voice. "Piles of paperwork..."

"Actually, now that you mention paperwork," Julie interrupted him, "I really ought to . . ."

Jordan gave her a level look. "You ought to have a nice, hot lunch. I think you've lost a little weight since you left D.C."

"No, I haven't."

"Now don't pout, Julie."

"I'm not pouting. I'm merely saying that I weigh exactly the same."

"Baby, I'm not criticizing. Believe me, you still look beautiful. Cast and all. I almost forgot how beautiful."

Julie felt the heat rise in her face. The gall of him. Coming on to her like that. In front of Ben, no less. What was his game? And then it hit her: his new show. Oh, this was priceless. Had he actually come here to woo her into taking on the coanchor spot? Now that she was in the networks' good graces again, was he ready to welcome her back with open arms? On all fronts? Well, she was definitely not interested in picking up where they left off as far as their affair was concerned, but she had to admit she didn't feel nearly as cavalier about a chance at a truly plum job. One thing she couldn't deny: If Jordan Hammond was involved in a project, it was bound to be top rate. No dialogues with dead people, no pooches, penguins or turkeys.

She felt a flash of guilt. What about "Pittsville Patter"? Then again, she rationalized, it wasn't as if she hadn't told everyone here—including Ben—that if something really great came along over the next few weeks, she'd have to seriously consider it. And there was no getting away from the fact that this could be the "something great" she'd been waiting for.

She had a lot to sort out. Things were moving too fast. The first thing was to put Jordan on hold.

"I'm really not hungry, Jordan," she said, feeling very uncomfortable about the way both men were observing her—Jordan with unabashed expectation and Ben with no readable expression at all on his face. "Maybe we could meet for coffee later. I'll give you a call. Where are you . . . staying?"

Jordan blinked several times. "Where am I staying? Well, naturally, I thought I'd stay with you, darling."

Julie was flabbergasted. Had Jordan taken leave of his senses? Did he have amnesia or something? They'd broken up. He'd dumped her. "With me? You thought—"

Her eyes shot to Ben. No trouble reading the expression on his face now. Sheer disgust was emblazoned like neon across his features. Without a word, he strode across the room like a man with a mission and headed for his door.

"Ben, wait. Where are you going?" she asked anxiously.

"I have to see someone about a dog," he muttered as he closed the door behind him.

Jordan smiled offhandedly. "Nice guy. I like his style."

Julie sighed. "So do I."

Jordan dismissed her remark with a casual nod. He reached out and stroked her cheek. "I missed you, Julie. Since you came up here I've felt so cut off from you. We used to share everything, Julie. We used to be close as two peas in a pod. I thought you'd at least write to me, let me know how you were doing."

"Are you serious, Jordan?" she asked incredulously.

"Of course I'm serious, darling. Granted, I knew you needed some time and space—"

"I wasn't the one that said I needed time and space," she retorted. "You were the one. . . ."

"One thing you can't accuse me of, Julie, and that's not being sensitive to your needs. Even when you yourself aren't."

Julie could only shake her head in amazement. Had he always been this dense? This oblivious? This . . . forgetful? Had he always twisted reality around to suit him? What was it she'd ever seen in Jordan Hammond? She drew a blank.

"Actually, Jordan, I do need a little time and space. Right now."

"You sound upset, Julie. I guess you must feel a little like you've been on a roller coaster this past month. I understand. Believe me. But listen, we've got a lot to talk about. This month hasn't been an easy one for me, either."

"Right. I heard about the show being canceled."

"Oh, the show," he said, waving it off. "I'm talking about something more important than that. I'm talking about us, Julie. You and me."

*What gives here?* she wondered. Did Jordan really believe they could pick up where they left off? Water under the bridge? Coanchors and lovers once again?

"Look, Jordan . . ."

He put his fingers to her lips. "Not now, Julie. Like you said, we need to talk when we have the time and the space."

That wasn't at all what she'd said, but she let it go.

He checked his watch again. A Rolex, naturally. "I'll tell you what. We'll talk over cappuccinos, say, at three. You still love cappuccino, don't you, Julie?"

"They don't have cappuccino in Pittsville, Jordan. They have coffee. Good old plain American coffee."

"You are upset. You're not still thinking I didn't go to bat for you, darling. Julie, I practically crawled on all fours begging Bill to keep you on. I even told our womanizing Senator Cooper a thing or two when I bumped into him at the Balmore Country Club."

"Since when did you become a member of the Balmore?"

"I didn't. I went there as a guest."

She nodded, not pressing to find out who the member was who'd invited him. Julie was sure whoever it was, she was very attractive.

"What exactly did you say to Cooper?" she asked instead.

Jordan grinned. "It wasn't what I said . . . in so many words. You could say it's what I didn't say," he replied, sounding very proud of himself.

Julie arched an eyebrow. Jordan hadn't lost his touch. He was still tops when it came to dodging issues, confrontations, and questions.

"Well, I've got to get back to work," she said, pivoting around clumsily on her crutches. In truth, she wanted to track down Ben and clarify a few things with him. But could she clarify everything?

Jordan followed her out of the office. "And I suppose I've got to find a place to stay. Unless you—"

"Larkspur Bed and Breakfast's very nice. It's on Maple Street."

"What about the cappuc— Sorry, the coffee? Are we on for three?"

Julie nodded. She told him she'd meet him at the Full Moon.

A SHORT WHILE LATER, Julie cornered Ben in a small copy room on the first floor. "What man? What dog?" she demanded.

"What's with the third degree?"

"Why'd you make some dumb excuse to run out of your own office?" she persisted.

"Well, I'm sorry to disappoint you, Jules. Next time I'll try to come up with something *smarter*."

"What is the matter with you, Ben? Why are you being so—"

"Dumb?" he finished for her.

She was going to say something more like "hostile," but he was starting to get her angry. "Dumb is right."

"Sorry. But we can't all be as smart as the Jordan Hammonds of this world."

"Oh, for heaven's sake, Ben. You're behaving like a child."

"My, my, Jules, we're just full of compliments today."

"I didn't invite Jordan here, if that's of any interest to you. And he certainly isn't staying with me. It's over between us, Ben."

"Is it?" he asked, brushing past her as he exited the room.

Julie sighed heavily, leaning against the copier. There was nothing dumb about Ben.

"THE COFFEE IS GOOD," Jordan said as Betty filled his cup for a second time.

Betty beamed at him. "Why, thank you, Mr. Hammond," she gushed. "I want you to know I watch your show all the time. I've never met a real live celebrity before." She flushed a little as she glanced over at Julie. "I mean one that wasn't born and raised here in Pittsville."

Jordan bestowed a smile on the waitress who stood there, coffeepot in hand.

Julie had to ask twice for Betty to refill her cup.

"Oh, sorry, Julie. I don't know where my head's at," Betty apologized, but as she poured the coffee into Julie's cup her eyes kept straying in Jordan's direction.

"Betty!" Julie shrieked, as the coffee ran over the mug, spilling first onto the Formica table and then dripping down onto her skirt. Her white skirt.

Betty apologized profusely as both she and Jordan tried to come to Julie's aid with a pile of napkins.

"Oh, your poor skirt," Betty said, as Julie finished blotting the coffee on her lap. Several large brown blotches remained. "I'm so sorry, Julie."

"I guess this just isn't my day," Julie muttered.

"Would you like me to drive you home to change?" Jordan offered.

"No, it's okay. I'm heading home for the day after we have our coffee. The show airs tomorrow night and I like to spend the evening before going over notes and stuff.

"And you won't sleep a wink," Jordan said, knowing her routine. "I was always convinced that's what made you practically ready to kill by the time we got on the air."

"Sleep—or lack thereof—had nothing to do with it," Julie argued. "I was simply never one to dodge the tough questions."

Jordan smiled benignly, effectively dodging the obvious innuendo. "Still the same old Julie."

"Did you think I might have changed?" she challenged.

He reached across for her hand. "I certainly hoped not," he said softly.

Julie withdrew her hand from his grasp. Definitely time to change the subject. And get down to the real reason for his arrival on the scene. "So, Jordan, tell me about your new show."

He shrugged. "It's still in the development stage. Nothing is set yet."

"Really." Now, why didn't she believe him? And why didn't he want to discuss it? Had word filtered through the rumor mill that she had turned down everything thus far? Did Jordan think he had to woo her back into his bed in order to woo her into his coanchor seat?

He cupped his hands around the white diner-style mug. "Let's not talk about work now. I'm on a two-week break and I really need this vacation. I need to unwind. I need to touch base with those things in life—those people in my life—that really matter to me."

Julie squinted at him. Maybe this wasn't an act. However shallow he might be, Julie was beginning to get the feeling that her ex-lover was serious about trying to patch things up between them romantically. Well, this was one romance she was going to nip in the bud.

"Jordan, there's something you should know. . . ." She was about to tell him that she and Ben were personally involved, but then she stopped abruptly. Wait a minute. Why did she feel that Jordan Hammond deserved an explanation? What right did he have to know anything about her love life? He gave up those rights when he dumped her. And no matter how he chose to twist what had happened between them for his own purposes, Julie knew the truth. When her name was mud in the industry, he'd wanted nothing to do with her. Now that all that had changed, he was Johnny on the Spot, ready to change his tune. Well, as far as Julie was concerned, he was whistling Dixie.

"What should I know?" he prompted.

"What?"

"You started to say there's something I should know."

"Did I?"

"That's not like you to space out," he scolded lightly.

She smiled faintly. "Maybe I have changed."

"AND NOW, NO SWEAT deodorant and Hair's Looking at You, America's favorite hair-care products, are proud to bring you the award-winning 'Pittsville Patter' with none other than your favorite host and mine, Ben Sandler . . ."

The camera came in for a close-up on Ben, who gave his signature high-five wave.

"And his fiery hostess who really packs a wallop, Julie Hart . . ."

The camera swung over to Julie. She did a little punching jab with her fist, thinking to herself, *If you can't lick 'em, join 'em.*

"Tonight Ben and Julie will be interviewing our own renowned handwriting analyst from Pittsville, Mr. Ross Halpern. . . ."

As soon as they cut for a station break, Julie turned to Ben. "This is ridiculous."

"You okayed Halpern," Ben remarked blandly. "If I recall correctly, you saw having him on the show as a great opportunity for you to expose that 'fortune-telling nonsense' as a sham. Personally, I don't see it as nonsense at all." He smiled dryly. "But then, disagreeing with each other is the name of the game, isn't it? Your key to fame and fortune."

"I'm not talking about Halpern. Or the show," she said, her voice etched with frustration. "I'm talking about us."

"So what you're saying is, we're ridiculous."

"The way we're handling this is ridiculous." She was being generous with the "we." It was the way Ben was behaving that was ridiculous.

"Come on, Ben," she cajoled. "We're grown-ups. We've got to handle this like mature adults."

"Handle what, Jules?"

Instead of answering his question, she asked one of her own. "Where were you last night? I called until well past midnight."

"I was working. I turned the ringer off on my phone."

"Meaning you didn't want to talk to me."

"Meaning I was working."

"Nothing's going on between me and Jordan, Ben. Nothing personal, anyway. You've got to believe me. As for any...career decisions I might make, well...that doesn't have to have anything to do with . . . us."

"Doesn't it?"

Before Julie could respond, Ben turned to Ross Halpern who had just come on the set. Gus was hooking him up to his mike.

"All set, Ross?" Ben asked cordially.

"I guess," the handwriting analyst replied, glancing uneasily at Julie. Then Gus nodded, stepped back and began the countdown. . . .

"A SCIENCE?" Julie gave a condescending laugh. "I wouldn't call fortune-telling a science, Mr. Halpern. I'd be a lot quicker to call it pure hokum."

"Palmistry happens to be a respected form of divination that has been practiced since ancient times, Miss Hart," Halpern said archly. "There has even been medical research done on palmistry. Do you know that a number of medical experts have concluded that it is actually possible to predict certain ailments in newborns using palmistry?"

"I didn't know that," Ben said. "That's fascinating, Ross."

"Oh, please," Julie said derisively. "I can just see teams of doctors standing around newborns examining their tiny palms with magnifying glasses and making erudite diagnoses."

"The doctor that delivered my Josh did just that," Halpern said huffily. "And my wife and I were both greatly relieved when Josh got a clean bill of health. Not to mention that both the doctor and I were able to forecast the type of child Josh would be. He clearly had an Action/Mental hand."

Julie rolled her eyes.

"No," Ben said enthusiastically. "You mean you can actually look at a hand and tell what type of personality a baby's going to have?"

"Oh, absolutely. I can look at any hand and give you a pretty good rundown on anyone's personality."

Ben held up his hand to the palmist. "What type of personality am I?"

Julie snickered. Both men ignored her.

"Let's see. What we look at here is the shape of the hand and the length of the fingers." He took hold of Ben's hand and studied it thoughtfully for a few moments. "Rectangular shape, prominent knuckles. Skin cool and dry. That fits very nicely into the Emotional type."

Julie laughed dryly.

Halpern's eyes fell on Julie. "I should mention that the Emotional type is the most complex personality type."

Ben cast Julie a sidelong glance. "Complex. Hmm."

"Someone who loves romance, is drawn to nature, finds raising a family both a strong need and a desired challenge," Halpern said. "Someone who tends to be nostalgic. Someone who goes out of his way to avoid social or work pressures, preferring peace and quiet, an easygoing pace."

Despite herself, Julie couldn't help but agree with Halpern's analysis of Ben. Still, she didn't buy that the palmist was getting all that from her coanchor's hand. Everyone who knew Ben or had watched him on his show long enough could deduce as much.

"They're also very strong on time-honored traditions and aren't particularly interested in pursuing new ventures," Halpern continued.

Julie narrowed her eyes. "Wait a second. Did Ben here have a little chat with you by any chance before the show?"

"Absolutely not," Halpern said firmly. "I have never met Mr. Sandler before. Naturally, I've seen him around town, but I don't believe we've ever spoken at all."

"Never," Ben confirmed. "So tell me more," he coaxed the palmist.

Halpern resumed his study of Ben's hand. "This is very interesting. I don't often see this blend."

"What blend is that?" Ben asked.

"Your fingers indicate that you're not pure Emotional. You're part Technical."

"How can you tell?"

"Your fingers are close together. Squared off. The thumb is low set."

"Doesn't sound good to me," Julie said facetiously.

"On the contrary," Halpern said smugly. "This points to Ben here being charismatically charming, warm, generous . . ."

"Are you getting all this down, Jules?" Ben quipped.

"And, when unimpeded, able to achieve great success."

Ben grinned.

Julie snickered.

"Looking next at the nails, which are broad and flat, I have to tell you that in the past, palmists believed people with nails like this were . . . a bit slow, intelligence-wise," Halpern said.

Julie laughed dryly.

Ben's grin disappeared.

"Now, however," Halpern went on, "palmists have come to see that people with broad, flat nails are actually very talented individuals. They tend to have surprising depth and creativity, a fine sense of rhythm. And they're very good lovers," he added with a twinkle in his eye.

Julie flushed.

Ben smiled broadly.

"Say, I'm doing all right. So, now that we know what a winning *personality* I am, what can you tell me about my future, Ross?" Ben asked.

"Right," Julie said with mock excitement. "Let's get on to the fortune-telling part."

"I fully believe that the hand is the pathway to our understanding our own destiny," Halpern said, his impassioned voice that of the true believer.

Julie looked down at her palm, tapping it. "These little lines tell it all, huh?"

Halpern squared his shoulders. "Not merely the lines. As I was showing you with Ben's hand, we must take into account all of the characteristics of the hand. It's size and shape, the texture—is it hard or soft? Dry or oily? The fingernails . . ."

"Right, let's not forget the fingernails," Ben said, showering Julie with a deliberately lascivious grin.

Julie glowered at him.

Oblivious to the interchange between the coanchors, Halpern continued in a pedantic voice. "Then we must look at many aspects of the lines themselves. The number, length, depth. The hand tells us about our personality, our character, our goals, and also about what may happen in the future—"

"Whoa," Julie interrupted. "*May* happen in the future? You mean you hedge your bets, is that it?"

"I mean," he said tightly, "that the lines in the hand change over time. I mean that we are not totally at the mercy of our destinies. Both major shifts as well as minor shifts in our life alter our hands. In other words, we take a hand in what happens to us."

Ben grinned. "A hand. I like that. Very symbolic."

Halpern gave Ben's hand another close scrutiny. "Do you see this here?" The palmist traced a line threading diagonally up Ben's palm.

"What is it?" Ben asked.

"Your career line."

"Oh, really," Julie muttered.

"What does it tell you?" Ben pressed.

"Well, see how it begins here at the base of the palm and then it starts to run up toward your middle finger?"

Ben nodded. Even Julie found herself looking on.

"But it's halted by this short, sharp line crossing it. See how it only crosses the career line, and yet doesn't dissect any of the other lines?"

"That's significant?" Ben asked.

"Oh, yes," Halpern said.

"Let me guess," Julie deadpanned. "He's at a crossroads."

"In a way," Halpern agreed. "Only we have to take note of this line here that springs up at a right angle to the career line just over what I like to call the stop sign. This signifies that you're going to move up significantly in your career, Ben. Or at least there is the potential there. But we come to another blockage line, which means you are ambivalent or possibly anxious about making that move up. There are pressures that you're fighting." Halpern's eyes fell on Julie.

Without warning, Ben snatched up Julie's hand. "What do you see here, Ross?"

Julie snatched her hand back. "I'll pass, thank you. Allowing a palm reading would merely be giving credence to something I believe is—"

"Hokum," Ben said, filling in the blank.

She smiled curtly. "Exactly."

Ben turned to Halpern. "I imagine you run up against this sort of thing all the time."

"You mean, people who don't believe in palmistry? Well, yes . . ."

"No," Ben said. "I mean people who are scared you might discover something about them that they don't want you to see. Possibly something they don't want to see themselves."

"Oh, really," Julie snapped. "That's ridiculous."

Ben gave her a challenging look. "Is it?"

"You're just trying to egg me on," Julie said. "I don't think you believe this palmistry nonsense any more than I do. You're just playing the devil's advocate."

"Name me one thing Ross here told me about myself that you think isn't true," Ben challenged, his eyes sparkling.

Julie's mouth twitched. "This is so dumb."

"Just from the quick glance of Julie's hand I got," Ross interjected, "I would say she's a strong Action type. Rounded, curved palm, slim nails, thumb and little finger at a wide angle. A pure one at that, which is very rare."

"Rare, huh?" Ben mused. "That's Jules for you. They tossed the mold after they made her. So what kind of a personality goes with an Action hand," Ben asked the expert.

"The Action-type personality is usually very good at getting what he—or she, in this case—wants."

Julie smiled deprecatingly at Ben.

Ben sighed.

"Intensely active, naturally," Halpern continued. "Easily bored, avoids tedious jobs. A lot of journalists have Action-type hands. People who are very forceful and blunt. The type who consistently voices strong opinions that have the unintended but nevertheless all-too-frequent effect of causing resentment."

"You put him up to this," Julie challenged.

"No way. It's all there in that pretty little Action hand of yours, Jules."

The palmist gave Julie an earnest look. "I should warn you that Action people are subject to burnout," he cautioned. "And I usually advise these types that they'll live longer and happier lives if they take time out to smell the flowers, so to speak."

Again, Ben caught hold of Julie's hand, taking too firm a grip to allow her to retrieve it. "Tell me about her career line, Ross."

Julie relented. "Okay, okay. Have your fun," she said cavalierly.

Halpern studied her hand, then looked up at her. "Your career line begins with a fork."

"A fork." Ben gave her a pitying look and tsked.

"What? That's bad?" Julie asked sarcastically.

"Well, it presents a serious problem for you," Halpern said. "It means you've got a foot in two worlds."

"Don't you mean a hand?" Julie said dryly.

"Can you tell in which world her feet and hands are going to end up?" Ben asked the palmist.

He examined her hand again. "It's not yet resolved." Again, his gaze fixed on Julie. "Right now, you're feeling torn. Forces are pulling you in two directions. One force is coming from outside of you, the other from within."

Julie felt a flicker of discomfort. "And?" she pressed, despite herself.

"See the tiny chained sections running through your head line?" He traced the line running across the middle of her hand. "This indicates that you are under a great deal of stress right now from feeling pulled in two opposing directions. Then we look at the fine hairlines that spring off the head line."

Again the palmist's eyes met Julie's. "You're very confused. And note the hanging head line branching off from your primary head line . . ."

"Do you see the line that tells you I think this is all quackery?" she quipped, but her voice had an edginess to it.

"The hanging head line indicates that you're having a great deal of trouble thinking straight."

Julie pulled her hand away. "I can think perfectly straight," she said defensively, avoiding both Halpern's and Ben's eyes.

"What's the matter, Jules? Our fortune-teller getting too close for comfort?" Ben murmured.

*August 16*

I cornered Mr. Halpern after the show and had him give my hand a look. He told me I had a Technical/Action blend, which, he assured me, was a particularly desirable blend. He was especially pleased to see that my fingers were short and widespread. I'd never actually seen this as much of an asset before. In fact I always envied Alice her long, slender, graceful fingers. I suppose it doesn't help that I bite my nails. Mr. Halpern said that people with hands like mine usually do great in whatever profession they choose and can handle a lot of stress.

The best part—wait until I tell Alice—is that I have "psychic" fingernails, which means, according to Mr. Halpern, that I have a highly sensitive intuition and tend to "sense" things about people without any real knowledge.

I'll tell you one thing I "sense": trouble ahead for Aunt Julie and Ben. But I guess it doesn't really take a psychic to "sense" that!

# 9

JORDAN ARRIVED ON Julie's doorstep at seven-fifteen the next morning. She tugged her robe closed as she gave him a groggy look. "What are you doing here at this ungodly hour?"

"I've been up since five," Jordan said jauntily. He looked like he'd just stepped out of *GQ*. What the well-groomed gentleman wears in the country. Perfectly pressed khaki slacks, navy polo shirt, tan crewneck sweater slung over his shoulders, the sleeves tied in front, cordovan penny loafers and navy socks. His expensive musk cologne wafted in the air. Julie had almost forgotten how much the smell of that cologne bothered her.

She frowned, focusing not on Jordan's appearance but on what he'd just said. "Five this morning? You've been up since five this morning?"

"That's right. I came by to take you to breakfast. I've got this craving for blueberry pancakes with real maple syrup. Betty over at the Full Moon told me they make the best in the county. And she wanted me to tell you that she'll pay the cleaning bill personally on that skirt. So what do you say, Julie?"

She yawned. "Why?"

Jordan looked puzzled. "Why? Because she feels it was her fault."

"No. Why did you get up at five in the morning?" In all the times she'd been with Jordan she'd never seen him up before ten in the morning; more often than not, he slept closer to noon. They had both been night people and late risers.

He rubbed his hands together vigorously. "I like the mornings. Sunrise. The peace and quiet. Sanitation trucks rumbling down the street. Not here, of course, but in the city. Mornings are a great time, Julie."

Now Julie was really stunned. She'd thought at first it was just being up in the country. Maybe there were no shades on his windows at the B&B and the sun streaming into his room had woken him up. "You mean you get up at five o'clock *every* morning?"

Jordan smiled broadly. "The crack of dawn. Invigorating. Gets the old juices flowing."

Julie yawned again. "Well, my juices just want to go back to sleep."

She started to turn away.

"Great show last night, Julie."

She looked back at him. "You watched it?"

"Of course, I watched it. Would I miss it?"

"You're putting me on, right?"

"How can you say that?" he said, wearing his wounded expression. "I told you the moment I saw you that I think 'Pittsville Patter' is a great show."

"It's a long way from 'News and Views.'" There was a touch of wistfulness in her voice. It was a long way from interviewing the attorney general to a fortune-teller.

"Traditional news-interview shows are a dime a dozen on TV now. CNN alone must have twenty or more. Then there are all the networks and other cable stations scrambling to get in on the competition. No, I think the public is feeling oversaturated with shows like that. As well as with those talk shows that focus in on perversions and other titillating junk."

Julie nodded slowly. Except for the one cross-dresser Ben had interviewed a while back, she had to admit that "Patter" didn't really fall into either of those categories. It was in a class all its own. For the first time, it struck Julie in more of a positive than a negative sense.

"This is the nineties, Julie. Marketing tells us that people want to get back to basics. They want to see real people on TV. People concerned with the everyday issues of their lives. Like arguing over whether their town needs a new running track, or getting down to the nitty-gritty of what normal, everyday men and women are looking for in a relationship. Like touching base with our spiritual core."

"And you think that's what 'Pittsville Patter' is doing?"

"Doing exceedingly well. I think it's going to serve as a model."

"Really? And you thought last night's show was...?"

"Great. Fresh, spontaneous, entertaining." His smile broadened. "That guy's quite a character."

Julie grinned. "Halpern? Tell me about it."

"No, I meant Ben."

"You're calling Ben a character?" she said defensively. It was one thing for her to say something derogatory about Ben; quite another for Jordan Hammond—of all people—to bad-mouth him.

"I meant it in a good way," Jordan assured her. "I was impressed. He knows how to play both ends against the middle."

"Where does that put me?" she asked wryly.

Jordan smiled seductively. "You're in a class all your own, Julie." He wagged a finger at her, his smile now teasing. "He did have you going there, though, didn't he?"

"Ben?"

"No. I meant the palmist."

"Oh, please. Don't tell me you bought that bunk?"

Jordan smoothed down his already perfectly smooth polo. "Actually, I've made an appointment for a reading myself."

"What? Give me a break, Jordan."

"That's your problem, Julie. You're too cynical."

"My only problem is that I need to go back to sleep." She turned and headed for the stairs.

Jordan followed her into the house. "I wish you wouldn't keep running out on me, Julie."

She spun around. "Me running out on you? Don't we have our tables turned, Jordan?"

"I'm trying to mend some fences here, Julie. You were so . . . irrational after you got axed from the show, that it was impossible to . . ."

Julie was incensed. "Irrational?" she charged.

"Come on, Julie. Does a rational woman cut up her lover's sports coat into a million pieces and mail it back to him?"

Julie put her hands on her hips. Okay, it was time to call a spade a spade. "Don't you mean ex-lover?" she corrected tightly.

"That wasn't how I saw it," Jordan insisted. "You misunderstood my intentions completely. I simply thought it would be better for you if I stayed away from your place for a few weeks to give you a chance to...get your bearings. I did phone you, Julie."

"Right. To see if you'd left that jacket of yours behind."

"That happened to have been an Armani. And one of my particular favorites."

Julie smiled triumphantly. "Yes. I know."

Jordan sighed. "But, as I told you, I didn't hold any grudges. Like that palmist so accurately read in your lines, you haven't been thinking straight. Not to worry. I actually found a very similar Armani—on sale—no less."

Julie could only stare at him in amazement. The man was completely dense.

"Let's just say," Jordan said earnestly, "that it was a misunderstanding on both our parts. What's important here is that since we've been apart, I've been miserable. I wanted to call you a hundred times since you left D.C."

"You didn't call me once," she countered.

"I was afraid you'd hang up on me. I wanted to give you time to . . ."

"Mend my ways?"

He shook his head. "No. You're being too hard on yourself, darling. Your ways are just fine with me. You were good for me, Julie. I didn't realize how good until . . ."

"Until you got hitched to Susan Smith? Professionally speaking, that is. Or was it more than professional?"

Jordan started to answer, but Julie waved him off. "No, don't tell me. I don't want to know."

He smiled seductively. "That's because you still care."

"No, it isn't, Jordan," she said quite honestly. The only good thing about Jordan's arrival on the scene was that it gave Julie the opportunity to resolve any slight remnants of romantic feeling that might have been lingering in her mind about him. She saw her ex-lover in a true light now. And it wasn't particularly flattering. Jordan was dense, insensitive, opportunistic, and completely self-involved. Marriage to him would have been a disaster.

Actually, she decided, there was another plus to seeing Jordan in this new light. Now, if she coanchored with him on his new show, there'd be no issue whatsoever of personal complications. Their relationship would be strictly professional, which she believed would be a big plus for the show. Not that she'd made up her mind yet about accepting the spot. It would mean leaving Pittsville. Leaving Ben? Or would she ever be able to convince him to come with her? Ben was almost as hot as she was now. Surely, he'd be able to land a spot of his own in L.A. or New York, or wherever Jordan's new show was based. They could be together.

Be together. Yes, that was what she wanted. She and Ben together. And that's when it fully hit her: She was in love with Ben Sandler.

"You're off somewhere, Julie," Jordan said, touching her cheek.

Julie blinked. "What?"

"There was nothing between me and Susan." His brow creased. "Or is it Susan and I?"

"Susan?" she asked blankly.

He chuckled. "You are jealous."

And then she remembered which Susan he was talking about. Susan Smith. "No, really, Jordan . . ."

"It's okay, darling. I'm glad you're jealous. It proves you still care."

"No . . ."

"I have to confess something to you. I know this sounds corny, but you really did inspire me, Julie. I feel I did my best work when we were together."

She smiled to herself. He was finally getting down to brass tacks. It was about time he came to realize what an asset she was as his coanchor.

"What are you saying exactly, Jordan?" Time to spell it out. Time to hit her with the big question. Would she take the coanchor spot on his new show? Not that she would give him her answer right away, but she certainly had a lot of questions. Where would they be taping? What was the format going to be? Who was going to be running the show? What kind of a contract were they talking?

Jordan took hold of her hands. He smiled nervously. "Julie?"

"Yes, Jordan?"

"Would you . . . ?"

"Yes?"

He cleared his throat. "That is, will you . . ."

"Jordan, just spit it out."

"Julie, I want you to marry me."

Julie stared at him, speechless.

"We talked about it for months. I thought . . . before the unfortunate business with Senator Cooper happened . . . that we were close to setting a date. Let's set one now, Julie. Let's do it right away."

Julie was flabbergasted. "I thought . . . I didn't think . . . I wasn't thinking. . . ." She shut her eyes. What was it that palmist had said about her having trouble thinking straight?

Jordan drew her into his arms. Julie was too stunned to resist. "I love you, Julie."

"What about . . . the new show? I thought . . ."

"We'll get to that later. First things first." He cupped her chin; his mouth was starting to descend.

Julie stopped his progress, putting her hand in his face. "Morning breath," she mumbled, scooting out of his embrace.

"I don't mind," Jordan murmured, reaching for her again.

She scrambled out of his reach. "No, really, Jordan. I'm still . . . half asleep. This isn't the time. . . . We need to sit down and talk. Really talk. A lot has happened. Things can't be the same. Well, they can in some areas . . . maybe, but not . . . in all areas. I need to go upstairs now and . . . brush my teeth."

Jordan smiled. "I really knocked you for a loop, didn't I?"

Julie glanced down at her palm as she scurried up the stairs. "Now, how did Halpern miss this line?" she muttered.

"I'll wait for you," Jordan called up to her. "We can go have breakfast over at the Full Moon."

BEN LOOKED UP FROM his newspaper as Julie and Jordan walked into the café a half hour later. Jordan gave him a cheery wave, ushering a reluctant Julie over to the booth where Ben was sitting.

Jordan slapped Ben on the shoulder as he slid in beside him, leaving Julie to sit across from "her two men."

"Well, I told you I'd do it and I did it," Jordan said to Ben with a wink.

Julie stared at Jordan. "What did you tell Ben? You didn't . . ." Her gaze shifted to Ben. "He didn't . . ."

Jordan grinned. "I've got her so flummoxed she can't even finish a sentence."

Ben's eyes were fixed on Julie. "So what did she say, Jordy?"

Jordan laughed. "Jordy. This guy cracks me up."

Julie had trouble pulling her gaze away from Ben, but her question was directed at Jordan. "Since when did you and 'this guy' get so chummy?"

"We had dinner together last night right here at the Full Moon," Jordan said convivially. "Great pot roast. Best I've had since I was a kid. And that roast chicken you had looked mighty good, too, Ben."

"Yeah, it was great," Ben said in a monotone. "So what did she say?" he repeated.

"Well, she didn't say no," Jordan chirped.

"Now wait a minute, Jordan," Julie said.

Ben folded up his newspaper. "Look, I'm sure you two lovebirds want to be alone—"

"Hey, we've got all the time in the world for that," Jordan said magnanimously.

"Jordan," Julie said tightly. He was giving Ben the completely wrong impression.

Jordan winked at Ben. "She always was impatient."

"Yeah, I know," Ben said.

Julie glared at them both. "That's it. I've had it. With both of you." She shot up out of the booth. "Men," she muttered, colliding head-on with Betty as she spun around to leave—Betty and a plate of sunny-side-over eggs and corned-beef hash. Her white slacks and mint green tank top decorated with somebody's breakfast, Julie stormed out of the café.

Jordan started to rise. "I'd better go after her."

Ben put a hand on Jordan's arm. "Take my advice and give her a little time to cool off. And clean up."

Jordan deliberated, then nodded after a few moments. "I guess you're right."

Ben took a sip of his now tepid coffee. Then he looked over at the man beside him. "So, tell me, Jordy. Besides popping the big question, did you tell her the rest?"

"IT ISN'T FUNNY," Julie snapped as she stood in the middle of Kate's office trying to scrub egg yolk and hash stains from her clothes.

Kate and Rachel both bit down on their lower lips. They could see their sister was close to tears.

"You're not going to get the stains out," Kate said softly. "I've got some stuff in my closet. You can change into one of my dresses. It'll probably be a little big on you but you can use a belt. . . ."

"I love him."

Kate, who was heading over to her closet, stopped short.

"Not . . . Jordan?" Rachel asked anxiously.

"Jordan? Of course not, Jordan. I love Ben."

Rachel broke out in a smile. "That's better."

Julie slumped into a chair. "No, it isn't. It's worse. It's awful. It's impossible. The man's incorrigible, impossible, irascible, and I'm completely nuts about him."

"So, are you still going to take the coanchor spot with Jordan?" Kate asked. As soon as they'd learned Jordan was coming to Pittsville, all three sisters had surmised that he was coming there to sign Julie on for his new show.

Julie's expression reflected her confusion. "No. I don't know. He hasn't even asked me yet. First things first," she said, mimicking Jordan's clipped Bostonian accent—a sheer invention, since he'd grown up in Minneapolis.

"What comes first?" Rachel queried.

Julie sighed wearily. "Marriage."

"Marriage?" both sisters repeated in unison.

"And what's worse, he discussed it first with his new chum."

Kate squinted. "His new chum?"

"Ben," Rachel guessed.

"How did you know?" Julie asked.

"Delaney saw the two of them eating dinner together at the Full Moon last night when he ran in there for a cup of coffee."

"Can you believe it?" Julie murmured. "Jordan is so dim, so oblivious. It didn't even enter his mind that Ben and I . . ." She exhaled loudly. "And Ben. He didn't say a word about . . . about us."

"Did you?" Kate countered. "Did you tell Jordan that you and Ben were . . . ?" She raised her brows and smirked, deliberately letting the sentence dangle as Julie had.

Julie frowned. "Well . . . no. Not in so many words."

"How many words does it take?" Kate retorted.

"Don't be hard on her, Kate," Rachel scolded lightly, putting an arm around Julie's shoulder. "This isn't easy for her."

Julie sprang from the chair. "I've got to tell him."

"I do think Jordan should know you're in love with Ben," Rachel conceded.

"Not Jordan. Ben," Julie said.

Kate was incredulous. "You mean Ben doesn't know?"

"Well, I didn't . . . I wasn't . . . There didn't seem to be . . ." Julie shook her head and gave her sisters a weak smile. "No."

IT TOOK JULIE HALF the morning to track Ben down. She finally found him swimming at Simon Pond, which ostensibly belonged to Ben's famous magazine-publisher neighbor, Ron Jamison, but Ben had told her that Jamison had encouraged him to feel free to use the pond anytime he wanted.

Julie watched Ben cut through the water for several long minutes, while she tried to get up the nerve to confess her true feelings to him. Their relationship had been so rocky and tempestuous since her return to Pittsville, and she knew it was going to be far from smooth sailing from this point on. Especially if she took the coanchor spot with Jordan.

For one insane moment she actually contemplated looking up Ross Halpern and getting a reading. Then she chided herself sharply and made her way on her crutches down to the edge of the pond.

"How's the water?" she called out to him.

Ben kept swimming, not even looking her way.

Had he heard her? "I said . . ." she started to shout.

He ducked under the water.

She kicked off her one sandal and rolled up the cuffs of her stained white trousers, having rushed out of Kate's office without bothering to change. Fortunately, her cast was one of those new plastic compositions and it wouldn't matter if it got a little damp. Using her crutches, she waded into the pond, trying to keep her broken leg up in the air.

"Ouch," she muttered as she stepped on a pointy pebble. The water was ice cold, and what with it being overcast and cool this mid-August morning, a shiver shot right up from her feet to her head.

"Ben, I need to talk to you!" she called out, standing ankle deep in the pond, her feet getting numb on the mostly smooth, sandy bottom.

Ben broke into a butterfly stroke in the middle of the pond. As he moved into the stroke, she saw his bare butt rise out of the water for a moment. Another shiver shot through her. This one had nothing to do with being cold.

She waded in a little farther, forgetting about her cast; the cuffs of her slacks were getting wet. "Ben, I'm not going to marry Jordan."

He dove under again.

When his head resurfaced, she shouted, "I don't love Jordan Hammond!"

He switched to a breaststroke.

She waded in a little farther. "Ben, would you please stop swimming . . ." One step, two steps. "And listen to me." Three steps, four . . .

"Oh!" she gasped as the rocky bottom suddenly disappeared beneath her feet and she found herself plummeting into deep water. She went under and came up sputtering.

Ben rolled over lazily and began floating. "There's a big drop," he drawled.

"Thanks for telling me," she replied, treading water and trying to push sodden strands of wet hair back off her face. Once she'd blinked most of the water out of her eyes, they came to rest on Ben's enticingly exposed body as he continued floating on the surface, just out of her reach. God, he was gorgeous.

He smiled wryly at her. "I don't think you should be getting that cast soaked."

Julie, who was still mesmerized by his body, flushed, averting her eyes. She swam back to shallow waters, settling down close to a large boulder upon which she propped her bum leg so the sun could dry the cast. "You could have said something to Jordan." She hesitated. "About us."

Ben rolled onto his stomach, dove for her crutches, then swam over to her with them. "I figured that was your responsibility."

"He showed up at my door at seven o'clock in the morning. He woke me from a sound sleep. He caught me off guard. I didn't think that was what he was going to ask me."

She frowned at him. "Anyway, why did he tell you he was going to ask me to marry him? He doesn't know you from Adam."

Ben shrugged. "It was one of those man-to-man things."

"I can't believe it. He watched our shows. How could he be so blind? Couldn't he see that we . . . that you and I . . . well, that we obviously have something . . . going?" Why couldn't she just spit it out? Why was it so hard to tell Ben exactly how she felt?

His eyes were riveted on her. "What exactly do we have going, Jules?"

Her heart started to race. "I think I'm . . . in love with you, Ben." The words were a bare whisper.

His gaze was unwavering. "You mean you're not sure?"

"No. No, I mean . . . that's not what I mean. I am . . . sure." Droplets of water fell from her wet hair and she kept blinking them away. She took a deep breath and her body shuddered.

"What do you want to do about it?" His voice was low and husky.

"Get out of these wet clothes, for one thing," she murmured, slowly, provocatively lifting her sodden tank top over her head. Ben took it from her, tossed it over to the shore. Her hands moved down to the waistband of her white slacks.

"Wait," Ben said.

The next thing she knew, he was diving underwater. She thrilled with delight as he undid her slacks and removed them. He didn't come up for air until he'd also stripped her of her white silk bikini panties and slid them over her cast.

"What great breath control," she said with a seductive grin.

He unclasped the front closure of her lacy bra. The material fell away, exposing her full, creamy breasts.

"Now what?" he murmured.

She flushed. Did she really have to spell it out for him?

Ben cocked his head. "Jordan hasn't told you about his new show yet, has he?"

She sighed. "Oh, so that's it. Okay, Ben, I admit I can't assure you I have no *professional* interest in Jordan. He hasn't told me about this new show of his yet, but I'd be lying to you if I pretended I wasn't the least bit interested, or that I don't know that he's going to ask me to be his coanchor."

"Julie..."

"No, let me finish, Ben. Even after I turn down his marriage proposal—which I certainly intend to do before this day is out—knowing Jordan, I doubt that will deter him from wanting to work with me again. Now that I'm suddenly being sought after, I'm sure Jordan is bound and determined to be the one to 'win' me. Besides, he already admitted I inspire him, et cetera, et cetera." She didn't want to lay it on too thick.

"Julie..."

"I know. You want to know what my answer's going to be. I don't know for sure yet what answer I'm going to give him, Ben. It depends in part on... Well, in large part on... where we stand."

"Right now we're standing—or in this case, lying—naked in a very cold pond."

"We could . . . warm each other up."

He smiled tantalizingly. "So impatient."

She splashed water in his face.

He splashed her back.

The splashing quickly degenerated into an all-out water fight, each of them getting in some good licks. Julie started losing ground because she began laughing so hard. Her head fell back, underwater. Ben ducked his head under, too. They both opened their eyes. They gazed at each other. Julie made the first move. She brought her lips to meet his.

She'd never kissed a man underwater before. A heady experience, especially as she'd had to hold her breath for so long. Finally, still not breaking the surface, they breathed air into each other's mouths until it filled their lungs.

They both gasped as they came up for air. Both felt light-headed.

"That was a first," Julie said breathlessly, bursting with desire for him, but this time determined not to rush it. She could be patient. She could . . .

He smiled at her as he tenderly drew her wet hair away from her face. "You drive me nuts, Jules."

"That's because you love me. Love makes a person nuts. You drive me nuts, too. That's how I know I was never really in love with Jordan. He never drove me nuts, Ben. I was good and angry when he dumped me." She stopped and gave a little laugh. "Talk about being nuts. Here I am finally owning up to the fact that Jordan did dump me, and he seems to think it was all a figment of my imagination. Anyway, when it was over between us, as far as I was concerned, I was mad. But I wasn't devastated. I was a lot more upset over getting axed from the show than getting dumped by Jordan. It all basically boiled down to pride."

He kissed her lightly on the lips, but then he drew away, his expression solemn. "About Jordan's new show . . ."

She silenced him with a return kiss, this one far more passionate than his had been. She fit her naked body against his, fit her arms around his neck. The water made them rock with the gentle currents.

Her tongue darted out in search of his, found it, greeted it eagerly.

As Ben's resistance ebbed, his hands moved to her hips, then slowly, sensually, slid up her rib cage and over her breasts.

Playfully, she pushed him. "We mustn't be impatient," she teased, stretching out on her stomach, propping herself up on her hands, with both her good leg and the one in the cast bent up behind her in the air.

He met her head to head, giving her a loud, wet kiss on the lips. She kissed him back.

"Roll over," he commanded huskily.

She turned obligingly, stretching both her legs out in front of her on the boulder, propping herself on her elbows. Her full, pert breasts pointed skyward as she arched up into the sun. She threw her head back, closed her eyes.

Ben leaned over her, his tongue sliding around a taut nipple, licking away the wetness. "Mmm. You taste good."

"No hurry. Take your time. It's never wise to rush through a meal."

He smiled, moving on to her other pink tip, taking it in his mouth and letting his tongue roll over it.

A tremor slid over her. "Oh, yes. Savor... every... bite."

His mouth roamed again, sliding down over her belly, her jutting hipbone. He licked droplets of water off each kneecap.

She giggled.

The giggle faded as he gently coaxed her knees apart and his tongue began a slow, sultry slide from her kneecap down along the inside of her thigh. He drew her up, closer to the shore, so that they were lying in only a few inches of water. All the while his mouth continued its ascent.

"Ohhh," she moaned as his mouth covered her, his tongue dipping inside her, slowly, languidly, as the gentle currents of the icy water lapped around them. Only neither of them was feeling any chill. They were burning up.

She felt his hands gripping her buttocks, lifting her. With a broken cry of abandon, she opened herself up to him even more, writhing against the erotic slow-motion movements of his mouth and tongue.

Julie could hardly breathe. "You're... driving me... crazy."

He slid upward, his tongue drawing a line of fever up her body. "That's because you love me."

"Yes. Yes."

He slid his tongue across her lower lip. Her own tongue darted out to capture his. She drew his tongue into her mouth. Tasting him. Tasting herself on him.

She entwined her arms and legs around him, letting her head drop back so that the back of her head was in the water. He moved on top of her. Her hands glided down his spine. She could feel all his muscles there tighten as he hovered over her.

He looked down at her and smiled.

She smiled back up at him. "Okay, I give. If you make me wait one more second, Ben Sandler, I'm going to explode and there are going to be pieces of me floating all over this pond."

"We can't have that. I like you too much in one piece." He breathed the words into her mouth.

And then he was inside her—where he belonged. Water splashed around them as their bodies thrust against each other in a rhythm that was completely theirs. It was as though they were melding with the water, pulsating with it; as if its currents were inside them and radiating from them in wave after wave.

# 10

THE STORY WAS IN THE television section of *Variety* that arrived at WPIT the next morning. A prominent article about a new daily early-morning network magazine show scheduled to begin in the fall—a blend of news, entertainment, and a special "down-home" feature each day about "ordinary people" designed to "capture the spirit, the humor, the foibles, and the fascinating tapestry of everyday life." Hosted by Jordan Hammond and an as-yet-to-be-named coanchor.

Julie read the article through a second time, then looked over at Kate. "Hmm. Now I know why Jordan's been getting up at the crack of dawn. He's in training for having to be at the set for makeup by six in the morning."

Kate, who had already read the article, nodded. "Sounds like this one's really big-time," she said quietly.

Julie stared down at the article again. "'A fascinating tapestry of everyday life,'" she read aloud. "I bet they added that segment to the show after the brouhaha about 'Patter.' And that's especially why Jordan came running down here to sign me on. I'm a natural for the spot."

"And you want it?" Kate pressed.

Julie compressed her lips. Did she want it? Did she want to appear daily on what had to be one of the premier spots for an anchor in daytime television. She could name a dozen top anchorwomen who would kill for the assignment. The exposure, the prestige, the money...

"Julie, listen to me," Kate said firmly. "If it's this syndication deal that's got you undecided, forget it. I've already talked to a backer who's willing to foot the bill for the production and distribution of the show with Ben alone, as the host. Naturally he'd prefer the two of you, but he does think Ben could pull it off on his own."

Julie kept staring at the article.

"It's Ben, isn't it?"

"I don't suppose this will come as a surprise to him," Julie muttered.

"If he loves you, Julie, he won't stand in your way."

"What I don't get is this waiting game Jordan's playing," Julie said. "Why not just come out and ask me if I want the spot? What's he waiting for?"

"Maybe he's still licking his wounds because you rejected his marriage proposal," Kate suggested.

"I suppose."

"You need to resolve this, Julie. One way or the other."

Julie nodded. "It says in the article that they're going to film in L.A. That's so far away. What if Ben...?" She sighed. "I know he could get an anchor spot out there, but will he?"

"You'll just have to ask him," Kate advised.

"Right. But first I've got to get a firm offer from Jordan. I don't want to go stirring anything up until I know just what kind of a deal we're talking."

"What if it's the deal of a lifetime and Ben refuses to go to L.A.?" Kate asked guardedly.

Julie's eyes widened. "I don't know. I just don't know. I guess I'll have to cross that bridge when I come to it."

She reached for the phone and dialed the bed-and-breakfast where Jordan was staying.

Wilma Mason, owner of the Larkspur B&B answered the phone and informed Julie that Jordan had gone off fly-fishing with Ben earlier that morning.

Julie hung up the phone. "I don't get it. Jordan and Ben are complete opposites. I can't believe they're becoming buddies."

Kate grinned. "You know what they say. Opposites attract."

TEN MINUTES AFTER Julie left Kate's office, Ben came barreling in.

"Where's Julie?" he demanded.

Kate looked up from her desk. "She's off looking for you and Jordan."

"Damn," he muttered, and stormed out, practically knocking Rachel down at the door.

He apologized profusely but rapidly before racing off down the hall to the exit.

"Where's the fire?" Rachel quipped.

Kate frowned. "I'm not sure, but I think I have an idea."

"You sound worried."

"I am," Kate said flatly.

JULIE FOUND JORDAN at Simon Pond trying to untangle his fishing line. Ben was nowhere in sight, which was a relief to Julie since she wanted to have a private heart-to-heart with Jordan.

"I just can't get the knack of it," Jordan said with a sigh as she approached.

"Where's Ben?" she asked.

"He took off a little while ago," Jordan said, giving up on the line.

"Jordan, we need to talk. Did you or did you not have your new show on your agenda when you came here to Pittsville?" she asked, getting straight to the point.

Jordan suddenly became absorbed with his tangled line again. "Well . . . yes."

"You came here not only to propose marriage but to make a business deal for the coanchor spot."

Jordan rubbed his jaw. "Julie . . ."

"Jordan, I hope you aren't going to let our current *personal* relationship stand in the way of our professional relationship. I read all about 'Here and Now' in *Variety* this morning. It sounds like a fantastic show. Let me cut straight to the chase, Jordan. I'm interested. I'd have to be out of my mind not to be interested. That's not to say I'm ready to sign on the dotted line yet. There are some things I have to work out first. . . ."

"Julie . . ."

"And of course I need to know exactly what kind of a deal you're offering. Now, I've never made any bones about resenting the disparity in salaries between male and female anchors, but I do acknowledge that you've been in this business a lot longer and, until the new show gets off the ground and builds a track record, you're obviously top banana. On the other hand, we both know I'm the one who can generate a lot of sparks. . . ."

"Julie, please."

"I know. I know. You don't want too many sparks. You don't want me pulling off the covers on the wrong people. But . . ."

"I asked Ben to coanchor with me."

"I'm not going to hold my punches altogeth—" She stopped in the middle of a word, as Jordan's statement finally sank in. She stared at Jordan, openmouthed.

"Julie, listen. . . ."

"You did what? You asked Ben to coanchor? My Ben?" Julie was in shock.

"Please don't take this personally. . . ."

"Don't take it personally? How am I supposed to take it? I turn down your marriage proposal and to get back at me, you ask my boyfriend to fill the spot you meant me to fill?" She was outraged.

"I didn't," Jordan said.

"You didn't what?" Julie demanded.

Jordan sighed. "I never meant for you to fill the spot, Julie. I came down here to hopefully accomplish two very important goals. One—the first and most important one—was to mend the fences between us and ask you to marry me. And the other was . . . to ask Ben Sandler to coanchor 'Here and Now.' It wasn't my decision alone, Julie. The producers thought he'd be perfect, too. His warm, down-home, amusing approach blends nicely with my more refined, sophisticated, wry style of interviewing."

Julie shook her head. "I don't believe this. You and Ben. Together."

"I want you to know you were the first one I suggested to the producers. But they felt you were a little too...controversial for a morning show. They wanted someone who was a little . . . cooler, more mellow. You understand. Let's be honest, Julie. You're anything but mellow. Not that you're not great—in the right setting. You're hard-hitting, incisive, impassioned, commanding. Terrific qualities, but not for a morning newsmagazine. We're going to be focusing on soft news. For folks to enjoy while they're eating their breakfasts. Before they have to face the stresses of the day. We don't want to start them off all wired up. And you have to admit, Julie, that your aggressive approach wouldn't be exactly soothing. Now, Ben, on the other hand—"

"What did he say?" Julie cut him off.

Jordan gave an uncomfortable little laugh. "Very insightful guy. Guessed right off that I was going to offer him the job."

Julie bit down hard on her lower lip. "He guessed? He wasn't even...surprised? You're telling me he knew you didn't want me from the start?"

"Like I say, I think he guessed. Especially after I explained that first day what type of show it was I was going to be doing."

"You told him about the show the first day you were here?" Julie didn't know who she was angrier at—Jordan or Ben.

"Just to feel him out. I didn't actually offer him the spot until this morning. To be honest, Julie, I knew you might be disappointed, but I thought if we were getting married and you were busy with all the preparations for the wedding and everything, that you wouldn't be too upset. Anyway, I know other offers have been pouring in for you, so it wasn't as if not getting this job would be all that much of a hardship. And I also thought if we were married it would be wiser not to work together. Let's face it, being together twenty-four hours a day can be too much time for even the best of marriages. And then, when you turned me down, it really hurt, Julie."

"Is that why you let me go on and on just now?" she asked, feeling completely demoralized. "To get back at me?"

"That's not fair, Julie. You didn't give me a chance to get a word in edgewise. I'd hoped, since I kept putting off talking to you about the new show, that you'd...get the hint."

She got it now. All it took was for a brick to fall on her head.

"You still haven't answered me," she said tightly.

"Answered you about what?"

"Did Ben say yes?"

Jordan cleared his throat. "Not exactly. Let's say we're in negotiations. You know how it is, Julie."

"Right. I know exactly how it is." For a few moments she stared off into the distance, not really seeing anything. Then without another word—what was there left to say?—she turned and began to head off.

"Julie, wait," Jordan called out, but as he started after her his foot got tangled in his fishing line and he went flying facedown to the ground. He cursed as he sat up and tried to disentangle himself. "Julie, don't be like this. I was hoping we could still be friends."

Julie just kept going.

TWENTY MINUTES LATER Ben was banging hard on Julie's front door. "Julie, will you just let me in so I can talk to you?"

He got no response.

"I know you're in there, Julie. I'm not leaving this doorstep until you let me in."

He banged some more.

"If you don't go away," Julie shouted from the other side of the door, "I'll call the police!"

Ben banged even louder. "Call them. I'm not leaving."

Five minutes later, a cruiser pulled up to the curb. Delaney Parker got out from behind the wheel and sauntered up the walk to the front door.

The police chief gave a nod of greeting. "Ben."

Ben nodded back. "Delaney."

"What seems to be the problem?" the chief asked laconically.

"The problem," Ben said evenly, "is your sister-in-law." He gestured with his thumb toward the front door. "She's the most stubborn, adolescent, hot-tempered—"

The door flew open. Julie was red-faced with fury. "I want you to arrest him this minute," she ordered Delaney.

"Arrest him for what?" Delaney asked.

"For disturbing the peace. For loitering. For being a public nuisance. For lying. For deceiving me.

For...for..." Without finishing, she slammed the door closed in both men's faces.

Delaney gave Ben a sideways glance. "She's not too happy with you."

"I drive her nuts." Ben shouted the words to make sure she could hear them.

"No, you don't," she shouted back through the door. "Not anymore."

Ben smiled at Delaney. "Do you believe her?"

"Nope."

Again, the door swung open. Julie glared at Ben. "It's over. Finished. I never want to see you again. Which I won't since you'll be in L.A. and I'll be here in Pittsville."

Delaney looked over at Ben. "You're going to L.A."

"Nope," Ben said.

Delaney turned to Julie. "He says he's not going to L.A."

"What does he mean, he's not going?" she demanded.

Delaney turned back to Ben. "What do you mean, you're not going?"

"I turned down Jordan's offer."

"He turned down—"

"Liar. He told me you were in *negotiations*. And I thought you weren't slick. What are you holding out for, Ben? A bigger salary? A nicer trailer? Other perks?"

"I'm not holding out for anything, damn it. I told Jordan no. *Nada*. No dice. Nothing doing. Do you want me to spell it out for you? *N-o*."

"Oh, that's great. Just great. I suppose that's supposed to make me feel better. I can hear it now. 'Oh, sorry, Jordan, but I couldn't do that to Julie,'" she mimicked Ben's laconic voice.

Ben looked over at Delaney. "What am I going to do with her?"

Delaney shrugged. "Beats me."

Julie turned on Delaney. "Whose side are you on, anyway?"

Delaney raised up his hands in surrender. "I'm a neutral party representing law and order."

"Well, then, do your job and throw him in the clink."

"I did not say, 'Oh, sorry, Jordan, but I couldn't do that to Julie,'" Ben insisted. "And I don't appreciate you putting words into my mouth, Jules."

"Maybe you didn't say it, but that's what you were thinking. What other reason would you have for turning him down?"

"What other reason? I'll tell you what other reason. I'm perfectly content to stay here in Pittsville and co-anchor 'Patter' with you. Okay, I knew you'd be upset when you found out Jordan didn't want you for 'Here and Now,' but that had nothing to do—"

Julie turned her head away. "I'm not listening."

Ben's features were rife with frustration. "Delaney, would you please tell Julie I didn't turn Jordan down to spare her feelings."

"He didn't . . ."

"Delaney, tell him I don't believe him."

"She doesn't . . ."

"Furthermore, tell him I absolutely think he'd be a total idiot not to take the job offer of a lifetime."

"She thinks . . ."

"Tell her I don't want the 'job offer of a lifetime.'"

"He doesn't . . ."

"Tell him I still don't believe him."

"She still doesn't . . ."

"And that I insist he take the job."

"She insists . . ."

"Tell her she can insist until she's blue in the face."

"You can insist . . ."

The door slammed shut again.

Delaney's lips curved in a faint smile. "She looked a little blue in the face."

Ben banged on her door again. "I haven't finished!" he shouted.

"Are you going to arrest him, Delaney, or do I call the state police?" Julie shouted back from the other side of the closed door.

Delaney sighed. "I think maybe you'd better cool it for a while, Ben. Come on. I'll buy you a beer over at Murphy's."

Ben stood there debating for a long minute. "Okay," Ben finally consented, but before he left he turned and gave the door one last bang. "I'll be back, Jules."

A window opened on the second floor. Both men looked up just as a huge pail of water came raining down on them. The pail itself followed, missing bopping Ben on the head by a hair.

"Arrest her, Delaney," Ben sputtered, wiping the water off his face with his hands. "Assault on an officer. Assault on a . . . a pedestrian. Do your duty, Chief."

Delaney threw up his hands. "Another second and I'm throwing the two of you in the clink. In the same cell. And I'll throw away the key and just let you punch it out until you both end up knocking each other's lights out," he muttered, storming down the walkway, water spraying everywhere as he shook his wet head vigorously.

Ben looked up at the window. "Now see what you've done."

"You mean what *you've* done," she snapped, pulling the window down so hard it was a miracle the panes of glass didn't pop right out.

"Okay, Jules. Fine. If this is the way you want it. When you come to your senses—if that's possible—you'll find me getting good and drunk at Murphy's."

There was no response.

DELANEY HAD GONE BACK on duty and Ben was on his third beer when Jordan showed up at Murphy's. He slid onto the next stool.

"Julie told me I'd find you here."

"Great," Ben muttered. "You, she's talking to. Me, I get the door slammed in my face and a bucket of water dumped on me."

"If it makes you feel any better, she wasn't exactly thrilled to see me." Jordan motioned to the bartender to bring him a beer.

"Why'd you tell her we were still in negotiations?" Ben demanded.

"I thought we were," Jordan said.

"I told you no. In no uncertain terms."

Jordan shrugged. "I figured you were just playing hardball. They all do."

"I'm not *them*." Ben took another swig of beer.

"I'm beginning to get that message," Jordan conceded.

Ben gave Jordan a long, thoughtful study. "You really love her?"

Jordan frowned. "I thought I did. I really did miss her. But now I'm beginning to think I missed a fantasy of who I thought Julie was. The real Julie . . ."

Ben's features hardened. "If you're going to knock her in any way, I'm warning you right now I'm likely to sock you in your nice, square-cut anchorman jaw."

"No, no. Nothing like that," Jordan assured him. "I guess the truth is she's . . . too much woman for me. All that spirit and fire. It's a lot to handle."

Ben smiled a little drunkenly. "Handling it is where all the fun is."

Jordan didn't get it. He shrugged, took a swallow of his beer. "Is there anything I can do to get you to reconsider?"

Ben shook his head.

"Well, I'll be around for another week. Maybe I'll come up with something."

"You won't," Ben said without hesitation. Then he finished off his beer.

"Let me buy you the next one," Jordan offered.

Ben shook his head. "No. Getting drunk isn't helping. I still feel lousy." He swiveled in his seat to face the celebrated anchor. "And I still think you're making a big mistake not bringing Julie on board for your new show. Before she came on 'Patter' it was as dull as dishwater. She was the one who—"

"Look, you don't have to sell me on Julie's talents," Jordan said, cutting him off. "In the right setting, the right time-slot, the right coanchor, she's dynamite. But like I said, for this particular show . . ."

"Yeah, yeah, yeah. I know," Ben said morosely. "It's just that I know how much she's hurting."

"You really do love her, huh?"

"No doubt about it," Ben said forlornly. He stared down at his empty glass mug. "Maybe I will have just one more beer. . . ."

THAT EVENING KATE and Rachel found Julie slumped in their father's armchair listening to a sad, bluesy Billy Holiday tune on the CD. A half-empty bottle of wine sat beside her on the cherry side table.

"Are you drunk?" Kate asked without preamble.

Julie rolled her empty wineglass between her hands. "If you mean am I drunk enough not to still be feeling miserable, the answer's no."

Rachel removed the glass from Julie's hand and snatched up the wine bottle. "This isn't the answer, Julie."

"I know," Julie confessed. "It was an open bottle I found in the fridge. I only had half a glass. I hate to drink. I hate feeling miserable. I hate Jordan Hammond. I hate the powers that be in the industry. I hate being in love. I hate . . ." She was about to say Ben Sandler. She wanted to say Ben Sandler. Somehow though, she just couldn't get herself to say Ben Sandler.

"How about some coffee?" Kate suggested.

Julie smiled wryly. "To sober me up?"

Kate grinned. "No. Because it'll give me something useful to do."

While Kate went off to the kitchen, Rachel lowered herself into one of the club chairs. She winced.

"Are you okay?" Julie asked, lifting herself out of her self-absorption.

Rachel smiled. "Fine. The baby just kicked. An active little tyke." She put her hand on her stomach. "There's another one. Want to feel?"

Julie came over and knelt beside Rachel, letting her sister guide her hand over her extended belly. When Julie felt the first kick, tears came to her eyes. "Oh, that's so incredible," she murmured in awe.

"It is," Rachel agreed, her smile radiant.

"Oh, Rach. You're so lucky. A great husband, a baby on the way, a job you love . . ."

"Hey, if you remember, I went through hell and back before getting so lucky," Rachel countered.

Julie set her crutches aside and sat on the floor. "Sitting here all afternoon, I thought about a lot of things. When Jordan first told me he'd asked Ben to coanchor his new show, I was devastated. And then when Ben told me he'd turned him down, it didn't make me feel better. It made me feel worse. Because I knew, no matter what he said, that he said no because of me. I lambasted him for refusing the career move of a lifetime because he thought I'd be shattered."

"Which you were," Rachel gently reminded her sister.

"I know," Julie said. "But I was wrong. If you really love someone, you can't let that someone throw away fame and fortune because your feelings are hurt. And the truth is, as hard as it is for me to admit it, Jordan was right. Ben would do a better job on a morning magazine show than I would. He's right for the spot. He's got that warm, easygoing, homey style. He can put a smile on your face, make you feel better about facing the day ahead. I'm too outspoken, too abrasive, too inflammatory for an a.m. show. I'd have folks choking on their breakfast cereal."

Kate, who'd come back into the living room carrying three mugs of coffee on a tray, laughed. "Not to mention the producers and the sponsors."

Julie rose to her feet with the aid of her crutches. "I've made a decision. I'm ready to sign on for a two-year stint for 'Patter.' That is," she looked at Kate, "if you still want me without Ben."

"Where's he going?" Kate asked.

"To L.A. If I have anything to do with it," Julie proclaimed.

Kate handed out the mugs of coffee. "I think you've got Ben all wrong," she said. "He's never once given me the slightest hint that he wanted fame and fortune, Julie. He's been hosting 'Patter' for three years—"

"Exactly," Julie interrupted. "He's in a rut. Even if he doesn't know it. This is a chance for him to really make a name for himself. A chance to be all he can be . . ."

"It's an anchor job," Rachel teased, "not the Marines."

Kate chuckled.

"No, I'm serious," Julie said. "I think Ben's just plain scared to put himself out there in the big leagues."

"What about your aspirations to be in the big leagues?" Kate asked.

"Anchoring a syndicated talk show is nothing to sneer at," Julie said. "And the more I've thought about it, the more I've begun to realize that's just the kind of quirky format that suits me. Instead of always being worried that someone's going to slap my hand—or give me the ax—when I go on the attack or say something controversial, I'll be applauded."

"The more controversy the better," Kate agreed. "That is, after all, what made everybody stand up and take notice of 'Patter.'"

"So, would you sign me on without Ben?" Julie asked again. "Not that I'd want to go it solo, but I'm sure we could scout around for a coanchor who would be a good foil. Maybe not as good as Ben . . ."

"I don't think that exists," Rachel mused.

"The answer's yes," Kate said. "But I think you're jumping the gun."

"Besides," Rachel said, "if you're staying on and you love him, why try to drive him out of town?"

Tears blurred Julie's vision. She sat back down in the armchair. "Because it's the . . . honorable thing to do. Because for the first time I'm thinking about Ben, not myself. Because being selfish and being truly in love with someone are antithetical." Tears fell into her coffee mug. "The only thing is . . . how am I ever going to live without him?"

Kate removed the mug of coffee from Julie's hand. "Maybe the wine was a better idea, after all."

# 11

BEN WAS NURSING a hangover the next morning when there was a knock on his door. Groaning, hands on his head, he made his way gingerly from his bedroom to the front door.

"Okay, okay," he croaked. "I hear you."

When he opened the door and saw Julie of all people standing there, he blinked several times to make sure he wasn't seeing things. If he was, he supposed it was better to see Julie than a pink elephant.

"If you want to slam the door in my face or dump a bucket of water on me, go ahead," she said contritely.

"If I slam the door in your face, my head just may explode."

Julie gave him a closer survey. "You look awful. Are you sick?"

He stepped away from the door, his fingers at his temples. "Let's just say I've felt better."

"I came over to apologize."

"Accepted," Ben said, shuffling toward the kitchen. "I need coffee."

"You need to go lie down," Julie said. "I'll make the coffee."

Ben didn't argue.

Ten minutes later, Julie arrived in Ben's bedroom with coffee, a glass of orange juice, scrambled eggs and toast. All on a tray balanced on one hand as she hobbled over to the bed on one crutch. At least she was now able, per doctor's orders, to put weight on the leg, which was in its new cast.

"And I didn't even burn the eggs," she said proudly.

Ben took one look at the food and turned green.

"Just how much did you drink last night?" she asked with a wry smile, setting everything but the coffee out of his sight.

He took a grateful sip of the coffee. "Too much."

"Should I come back later?"

His hand shot out for her. "No. No, don't go."

She sat down on the edge of the bed. "Ben, I came here to tell you that I really want you to take Jordan's offer. It's a great opportunity for you. Why, you'd be right up there with guys like Gumble, Brokaw...."

"Hammond?"

"You'll outshine Jordan by a mile," she said softly. "You do already."

"Julie, I told you . . . Or at least I tried to tell you . . ."

"I admit at first I was jealous and resentful. But I'm not now. I don't want to hold you back. And, if it makes you feel any better, I realize it isn't the kind of show for me."

"What about us? What happens to us if I go off to L.A.?"

"I . . . don't know," she admitted. "I guess we'll have to see how we both feel once you're out there making a name for yourself."

Ben set aside the coffee cup and took hold of her hands. "What do I have to do, Jules, to convince you I've got everything I want and need here in Pittsville?"

"You're just scared, Ben. Wasn't that what that palm reader said? He saw a big career move in your future but believed your own fear and anxiety would keep you from making the jump."

"So, all of a sudden, Halpern's not a quack? All of a sudden, you're buying what he said?"

"No, I'm just saying I'm not the only one . . ."

He gripped Julie by the shoulders, ignoring the pain in his head. "Julie, I love you."

"I love you, too, Ben. That's why I don't want to be the one to stand in your way."

Ben released her and let his head fall back against his pillows. "You really are driving me nuts, Jules."

"Look, Ben. Once you're out there and you've gotten your feet wet, if you still feel I'm driving you nuts..."

He gave her a lingering look, then smiled. "If I have my way, Jules, you're gonna be driving me nuts for the rest of my life."

LEO HART AND MELLIE arrived home from Connecticut on Wednesday afternoon. Rachel, who met them at the train station, immediately hustled them off to Kate's office at WPIT for a secret briefing. Also in attendance were Skye, Delaney, Meg Cromwell, and the two special guests for that evening's "Pittsville Patter" show.

While the closed-door meeting at WPIT was going on, Jordan Hammond was waylaying Ben at the Full Moon Café, presenting him with what he insisted was his "final offer."

"It's nothing to sneeze at, Ben," Jordan said after concluding his pitch.

"I'm not sneezing, Jordy."

"You mean you'll accept the offer?"

Ben smiled. "No. I'm just not sneezing."

Jordan sighed. "Okay, tell me what you want. I can't promise I can get it for you, but you tell me and I'll see what I can do."

Ben swallowed the last bite of his turkey sandwich and slid out of the booth. "I'll spell it out for you. Tonight."

Jordan frowned. "Tonight? When tonight?"

"Eight o'clock."

"Eight . . . But that's when you go on the air."

Ben winked. "Stay tuned."

IT WAS TEN MINUTES before airtime when Julie was informed that Dick Janson, the fireman/poet scheduled for that night's show, had called in sick.

"Appendicitis," Kate said.

"So, now what do we do?" Julie asked with undisguised anxiety. "I'm not going to spend a half hour on the air with Ben without a guest. It would be too . . . intense."

"Not to worry. I got someone to fill in for Janson," Kate assured her.

"Who?"

Before Kate could answer, Skye—right on schedule—popped into her mother's office. "Mom, Gus has to see you on the set. On the double. Some problem with one of the cameras."

"Oh, great," Kate muttered with exaggerated agitation. "If it's not one thing, it's another," she said, hurrying out of the room.

"Wait," Julie called out. "You didn't tell me . . ."

Skye hung back by the door. "I don't think she heard you."

Julie looked over at her niece. "I don't suppose you know who our guest is tonight."

"Gee, sorry, Aunt Julie. I have no idea. Shame about Mr. Janson coming down with arthritis at the last minute like that."

Julie's eyes narrowed. "Your mother said it was appendicitis."

Skye fidgeted. "Oh, right. Appendicitis. I always get those two confused."

Julie was beginning to smell something fishy. "You wouldn't want to tell me what's going on here, Skye Hart."

Skye smiled innocently. "Gosh, Aunt Julie, I have no idea. I mean, I'm not psychic or anything."

THE SIGNATURE THEME music came on with a familiar blast. To Julie's own amazement, the tune had actually grown on her and she no longer wanted to change it. The music was lowered as the show's announcer, Allan Harper, began the intro. "And now 'Ecstasy' Perfume, the scent of the stars, and Lexor Cameras—'Turn an event into a lasting memory'—are proud to bring you the award-winning and soon-to-be-nationally-syndicated show from right here in our own backyard, 'Pittsville Patter,' with none other than your favorite host and mine, Ben Sandler . . ."

The camera came in for a close-up on Ben, who gave his signature high-five wave.

"And his fiery hostess who really packs a wallop, Julie Hart . . ."

The camera swung over to Julie, who did what had now become her trademark punching jab.

"When we return, Ben and Julie will not only be interviewing their guest, George Calhoun of Calhoun's Formalwear—'For those occasions when you care to wear the very best'—but they've generously agreed to wear a lovely gown and tux from his shop to give their viewers a firsthand look at what you might find when you visit the Calhoun showroom on the corner of Nichols and Elm. Don't go away, folks. This is one 'Patter' you're not going to want to miss."

"You've got to be kidding," Julie said to Ben as they cut away for a commercial.

Ben was already stripping off his shirt, and two dressers from Calhoun's came rushing out with a gown for Julie. A white lace gown. Meanwhile, a stagehand set up a screen so Julie could have some privacy to change.

"This is ridiculous," Julie argued, while one dresser was pulling her blouse off her shoulders and the other was unzipping her skirt. The whole time, Julie kept trying to balance on her crutches.

"One minute ten!" Gus shouted.

"I feel like I'm going to a prom," Julie muttered as the white lace gown was being slipped over her head. "Or a—" She stopped short, giving the gown a closer examination. "This is a wedding dress."

"Calhoun's is famous for their wedding gowns," one of the dressers told her as she plucked off Julie's one beige sandal, exchanging it for a white satin flat.

"At least the white matches your white cast," the other dresser said with a smile.

"Whose dumb idea was this, anyway?" she called out to Ben, but she got no reply.

"Thirty seconds," Gus cried. "How are we doing?"

Ben was slipping on his tails. "Great. I feel like Fred Astaire."

The two dressers drew away the screen. There was Julie standing in an exquisite off-the-shoulder white floor-length gown of satin and lace, supporting herself on her crutches. Kelly, the makeup girl, rushed over to her and quickly applied some more blush and lip gloss.

"Gosh," Kelly said moonily. "You make a beautiful bride, Julie."

Julie rolled her eyes. "I feel like an idiot."

Then her gaze fell on Ben, looking drop-dead gorgeous in his black tux. She smiled tremulously. "We'd make good models for the top of a wedding cake."

"Five, four, three, two, one..." Gus counted off.

George Calhoun and a second man, who was introduced as Daniel Bloom and whom Julie assumed was Calhoun's assistant, entered and sat down at the round table. George started off by describing in detail the outfits Julie and Ben were wearing.

"Julie's gown is a one-of-a-kind design by Gisella Reneau, who lives right here in the Berkshires," George was saying. "In fact, it just came in this morning so this is the first time it's ever been worn." He turned to Julie, who felt like a complete fool sitting in her captain's chair dressed like a bride with one leg in a cast, no less, and trying to look like a dignified anchor. "And may I say, Julie, that gown was made for you."

Julie smiled awkwardly. "Thanks," she muttered.

Ben turned to Calhoun. "So, tell me, George, what's the most unusual or outlandish wedding you've been involved in up to now?"

Calhoun pondered the question for a few moments. "Well, last year I had a couple who said their vows while floating down from the sky in parachutes. The poor minister was a nervous wreck because it was his first jump. But it came off without a hitch."

Julie eyed the gray-haired man sitting quietly next to Calhoun. "And what about you, Daniel? Are you with Calhoun's Formalwear?"

"Oh, no," Daniel Bloom replied with an amiable smile.

"But you are in the . . . 'wedding game,' as Ben calls it?"

"Getting married isn't a game, Julie," Bloom said with a gentle smile. "It's a very serious business."

"You're absolutely right," Ben said. "Whether you're saying your vows while you're dropping down from the sky in a parachute or whether you're on a television show."

Julie's mouth dropped open.

Ben grinned at her. "For such a smart woman, Jules, you've been awfully slow on the uptake."

Out of the corner of her eye she saw people start to filter onto the set—Kate, Skye, Rachel, Delaney, her father, Mellie, Ben's sister, Leanne, and her husband and baby. They were all dressed to the nines.

"You've . . . got . . . to be . . . kidding, Ben," Julie stammered.

She saw Daniel Bloom draw a book out of his inside jacket pocket. A Bible.

All three men rose and pulled the table out of the way. Julie just sat there in her chair, too stunned to say anything.

Ben wore a tender smile as he slowly approached her and dropped to one knee in front of her.

"Ben, don't do this," Julie said, sotto voce, trying not to move her lips.

He took hold of her trembling, clammy hand. "Jules, I've loved you since that first day I set eyes on you in grade school. All these years, no matter who I dated, it could never be the real thing for me. You're the real thing, Jules. And all it would take to make me the happiest, most successful man on this planet, is to spend my life with you here in Pittsville—off the air and on the air." He pulled out two sheets of paper from his pocket. One was a marriage license and the other was the contract for 'Pittsville Patter.' Both papers bore his signature.

Julie blinked back tears as she stared at the papers. "Oh, Ben . . ."

"Will you marry me, Jules?"

Julie opened her mouth but she couldn't get any words out.

Gus came onto the set. He'd slipped on a sports jacket and slicked back his hair—a first for Gus.

"Okay, wait. Before you give me your answer I just want to call one more person onto the set," Ben said, still holding Julie's hand.

Her eyes widened as Ross Halpern stepped forward. He came over to Ben, who ceremoniously handed Julie's hand over to him. Julie was too dumbstruck by everything that was happening to protest.

"So, what do you see in the love-ever-after department, Ross?" Ben asked the palmist.

Halpern studied her hand thoughtfully, nodding to himself. Meanwhile all the "wedding guests" had gathered around Julie's chair.

"What?" Julie said finally. "What do you see?"

Halpern traced a horizontal line on the side of her hand, that ran under her pinkie. "This is the affection line," he explained. "This line gives us a clear indication of the depth of one's feelings for someone else. Now, see how this line droops downward as it moves onto the palm. This indicates that you have ended one relationship. But as we move to the line right beside it—" he traced the new line with his finger "—we see a different story altogether."

Julie looked at him quizzically. "We do?"

Ben leaned closer. "What's the story, Ross?"

"See how deep this line is. How it reaches a good half-inch into the hand?"

Both Ben and Julie nodded.

The palmist's eyes lifted to Julie. "This means that you are now in a relationship that holds very deep meaning for you and will be long lasting. Now, as I pull the tip of your pinkie sideways, we see that this line actually is even deeper than it first appears."

"So?" Julie prompted, completely buying into the reading at this point.

The palmist smiled warmly. "I always say if you have a line like this, you are truly blessed. It's one of the real rare ones. What some, including myself, might say, signifies the 'perfect' marriage."

Julie looked down at Ben, who was still poised on one knee.

He was smiling up at her. "The perfect marriage. The perfect show. It's written right there in your hand, Jules."

Julie's face broke into a slow grin. "You know what I think of this fortune-telling nonsense?"

He cupped her face in both hands and kissed her while the palm reader was still holding on to her hand. When they broke away, Halpern handed her hand over to Ben.

Ben laced his fingers with Julie's.

"Oh," Halpern said, "about how many children you'll have . . ."

"Three," Julie said, her smile deepening.

"I guess that settles it," Ben murmured, rising and then bringing his bride-to-be to her feet to the cheers of all the wedding guests. Down at Murphy's, and over at the Full Moon Café, where large crowds were gathered around the TVs, more cheers broke out. Betty dabbed at her eyes with the edge of her apron. Jordan sighed and tore up the contract he'd hoped he could still talk Ben into signing.

Gus cued Mike in the control room and "The Wedding March" poured from the speakers.

Daniel Bloom, who turned out to be the minister of the Unitarian Church, took his position at stage left. The guests formed into two rows and held up their arms, forming an arch.

Ben tossed aside one of Julie's crutches and slipped her hand through his arm.

"You know," she said, "we'll probably spend the rest of our lives driving each other nuts."

He grinned. "I'm counting on it."

He drew her into his arms and kissed her for so long that Gus had to hurry over and tap them on their shoulders. "Come on, guys. We've got three minutes to pull this off before we have to cut to a commercial."

*August 24*

And didn't I predict that Ben would ask Aunt Julie to marry him on television! Okay, so my psychic powers are still developing and I didn't see that they'd actually tie the knot on the air. Psychic powers aside, not only was Aunt Julie's televised wedding to Ben one of the neatest weddings I've ever been to, but it got higher ratings in the broadcast area than any of the network shows airing at the same time. And the tape of the wedding show is going to be the first "Pittsville Patter" to be aired for syndication—even though, during the actual ceremony, Aunt Julie got clobbered by the boom and blacked out for a second; good thing she'd already said, "I do."

Now that WPIT is finally going to get out of the red, Mom's looking for a new, forward-thinking, innovative program director. As for me, I'm on the lookout for a new, forward-thinking, innovative husband for my mom. She's the only Hart girl left without a spouse. She acts like that's just fine with her, but I know different.

There's only one hitch. Well, two. One is that my mom is dead set against falling in love. But the bigger hitch is that if Mom does get married again, she could lose WPIT. Turns out, according to the divorce decree, the station's up for grabs if Mom remarries. Which really sucks, especially since my dad's mom, Grandma Agnes—I'm not supposed to call her 'Grandma' because she says it makes her feel too old; just Agnes—has been itching to get control of the station ever since my mom took it over. If that happened, not only Mom, but very likely Aunt Rachel and Aunt Julie, could kiss their jobs goodbye.

It doesn't seem fair, which is exactly what I said to Brody Baker. Oh, right. I haven't written anything yet about Brody. Well, the truth is it would take up a whole journal to write about Brody Baker. And right now I've got to go off and do some back-to-school clothes shopping—ugh! But I'll get to Brody soon. With some very interesting predictions, as well. So, stay tuned....

* * * * *

*Look for Kate Hart's story in*
HEART TO HEART,
*available in October 1995 from Temptation.*

This month's
irresistible novels from

**HEARTSTRUCK by Elise Title**

Second in *The Hart Girls* trilogy

Julie Hart had reluctantly agreed to co-host a TV talk show with heart-throb Ben Sandler. The ratings soared as she challenged the guests and even ended up hitting the charming Ben! But there was no denying the chemistry between them, both on *and off* the set.

**MAD ABOUT YOU by Alyssa Dean**

Faye—an innocent, lost in the big city—had charmed Kent MacIntyre, until she had stolen his files. He found her hiding place only to learn that she desperately needed his help. A world-weary, cynical investigator, Kent knew damn well not to trust any woman. Why did he so want to believe her?

**UNDERCOVER BABY by Gina Wilkins**

Detective Dallas Sanders had taken part in some unusual undercover operations, but cracking the baby-smuggling ring was the toughest. Especially since it meant playing the part of an unwed, pregnant woman. Even worse, she had to pretend to be head over heels in love with no-good Sam Perry.

**PLAYBOY McCOY by Glenda Sanders**

Laurel Randolph had all the "facts" on McCoy. But she pushed aside any nagging doubts when she embarked on a shipboard fling with him. Under the hot tropical sun, McCoy made her feel sexy...desirable...loved. But was it the real thing?

Spoil yourself next month
with these four novels from

**HEART TO HEART by Elise Title**

Third in ***The Hart Girls*** trilogy

Kate Hart had had too many run-ins with Mr. Wrong and she would be darned if she would let Brody Baker smooth-talk his way into her heart...and into her bed. No matter *how* sexy he was!

**THE TROUBLE WITH BABIES by Madeline Harper**

Cal Markam was Annie Valentine's toughest case. She was hired to mould the millionaire playboy into a conservative company president, but a rumour was circulating that he had fathered twins! A man like Cal could only mean trouble. Double trouble.

**SERVICE WITH A SMILE by Carolyn Andrews**

Sunny Caldwell was determined to succeed and had two golden rules—to put her personal delivery service first and never to get involved with a client. She followed her rules until the day she met Chase Monroe and his needy family.

**PLAIN JANE'S MAN by Kristine Rolofson**

Plain Jane won a man. Well, not exactly. Feisty and independent Jane Plainfield won a boat. The man, gorgeous boat designer Peter Johnson, just seemed to come with it!